The Red String

D. Marie Prokop

当天神

Dedication

In memory of my mother, Mary.

It is all for the bright!

— D. Marie

ACKNOWLEDGMENTS

Thanks to my dear family, who supported and encouraged me, and sacrificed their precious computer time for me to finish my story. (We had to share one laptop between the four of us...what a world!) To all the doomsday pundits in the media, thanks for stirring the pot of ideas in my head. Out of these thoughts, the Guardian was created and my hope revived. To NANOWRIMO- you rock! Thanks to my Mandarin-fluent friends for helping to clarify language issues.

Most importantly, thanks to the Author of my life's story for giving me inexplicable inspiration and grace. I am eternally grateful for my own rescue.

CONTENTS

1 The Boy Meets Girl

Winter, 2053

"Are you sure?"

Dr. Jay Griffin glared up at the servile man in the grey suit in front of his desk. It was 4 p.m. He was beginning to get hungry and the coffee in his stomach had become harsh acid, sloshing around his ulcer. Hunger and pain aren't incentives for patience - especially not for someone as accustomed to having his way as the great neurosurgeon Jay Griffin. He shoved away the empty ceramic cup as if to punish it and stood up.

The visitor involuntarily flinched and took a tiny step back. Then he cleared his face, reset it with a calm exterior and straightened his back.

The doctor growled, "I don't have to remind you of my views on mistakes, Mr. Reynolds, do I?"

He didn't.

Reynolds had failed Dr. Griffin once before and had lived the rest of his life in regret. He had lost something very important to him because of that one mistake. Now he never made a move for Griffin without being absolutely certain. When the doctor had ordered him to find the right candidate, after being dissatisfied with everyone else's attempts, he knew he couldn't fail. He had done everything he could possibly do in order to follow the doctor's orders perfectly.

"Sir, I am positive. I have found the perfect candidate. She meets all the criteria you stipulated in your request," Mr. Reynolds paused. "And she accepted immediately."

"Really?" The doctor's eyes widened. "What did you have to do? Threaten her? Or...was she simply impressed by your overwhelming charm?"

The ruggedly dark and handsome doctor was greatly amused at his own joke, but after seeing Reynolds was unfazed, retracted his strong jaw muscles, causing his smile to disappear.

"She is under the impression she has been selected at random. She considers herself 'lucky', sir," Reynolds relayed, ignoring the doctor's jibe.

After all these years, Stanley Reynolds still worked for Griffin, powerlessly watching this genius doctor get a warped enjoyment out of having his guinea pigs come to him unaware that they were just that- guinea pigs. It was twisted. He had always known this about Griffin, but this time, it especially bothered Reynolds.

"We shall see how 'lucky' she is! All of the other subjects were not. When will her transfer be complete? It says here that she has been evaluated by Dr. Sparks for only two weeks. Do you really have all the information? Time is now of the essence- I am on a deadline! There is no way I can start over with a new candidate if this girl doesn't work out! Do you understand me, Reynolds?"

"Yes, doctor. All the tests came back with the desired results. For example, as you requested, her epilepsy is genetic- not caused by an accident or illness. Also, she has not been implanted with a chip. The benefit is clearly in your project's favor. There are no living relatives with the exception of her father, but he is a

2

factory worker with minimal education. He was a bit unsure about the opportunity, but she begged him. It is unlikely he will pose a problem for you in the future. If he does, I will personally take care of it. I must warn you, though, she is an unusual child. She's quite...spirited."

Mr. Reynolds still held no expression on his pale face as he deftly handed the computer pad over to his superior. The doctor took it and promptly touched the screen to open the file. The holographic image of Ainsling Anne Reid, age 16, appeared before them.

A slender, blond teenage girl with a dozen or so freckles painted boldly on her ivory face grinned self-consciously and gave an awkward giggle. She held up a small hand, as white as her face, and waved wildly at him.

"Hi, I'm Ainsling!"

She spoke cheerfully, full of optimism. The clip repeated. Reynolds, of course, gave no further comment. Dr. Griffin's eyes studied the replicated miniature image of Ainsling and he smiled slowly. He clicked the device off and gave a full grin to Reynolds.

"She is quite spirited... but only I can make her a *spirit*."

***

"Li! Are you coming or what?"

"Shut it- I'm on my way! What color is it tonight?"

"Ma-gent-a," related his friend Carlos, with clear, Spanish vowels.

Now that he had the password, Li hustled towards the Metro Bullet Station. He pulled his jacket up higher on his neck, wishing he had a scarf. His long, thick hair covered his collar, but the chilly wind from the lingering winter was determined to get through.

Before leaving his condo he had rubbed some ointment on the half-healed cuts on his bruised hand from the fight he'd gotten in last night. Tonight he was going to have to make a better effort at keeping his cool. If he succeeded, Carlos would be relieved. He was constantly annoyed at Li for dragging him into yet another fight. He claimed it was always right when he was about to dance with "the most beautiful girl in the world."

Whatever.

Carlos was a lover, not a fighter. Unlike Carlos, who was enamored with every girl he met, Li had never met a girl who could really impress him. In his opinion, girls turned out to be either self-centered and petty or conniving and shallow. Either way, they were trouble. Carlos could have them all.

Li went to the clubs to check out the music. It was the only thing he really cared about these days.

Inevitably, people got in the way. There were always those ignorant few who simply resented his face. His almond-shaped eyes got him into more trouble than his mouth ever had. That was all it took for him to get pushed around or mocked. Carlos lectured him to ignore their taunts, but he couldn't do it. At least this way, he was able to keep his martial arts skills sharp.

It was now 8 p.m. and darkness had settled down on the city. The #5 Metro Bullet pulled into the station and Li embarked on his journey. He arrived at his destination in less than two minutes. It was hard to imagine the days when automobiles, taxi cabs, trucks and motorcycles cluttered the city streets.

Carlos said 'magenta', huh? He began programming the card he had brought to get into the warehouse/club near the harbor when his Com started to sing out a ruckus anthem. He looked for the caller's identity.

'The Devil,' he read on the screen.

"What does that bastard want now?" he muttered in frustration. *"Da fu!"*

He barked the Mandarin word for "answer" at the voice-activated Com his father had given him and followed up with a curt, "What?"

"Is that any way for the son of a distinguished medical pioneer to answer his Com?" the voice asked.

"Well, *Doctor Pioneer*, I don't really give a-"

"Li, I need you to come to the clinic right now! I have a special job for you."

Li's eyebrows went up. His father sounded… well, *excited*. That was new. And a little creepy.

"Now? What for?"

"Stop asking questions! Didn't we have a deal? If so, get your butt down here!" his father demanded.

"Wan bi!" The call disconnected automatically at the sounds of the Mandarin word for "end."

Li cursed under his breath and kicked a nearby recycling bin. He was regretting the agreement he had made with his father to work for him at the clinic in exchange for providing him with his own place.

After getting kicked out of four boarding schools in four years, not many universities wanted to take a chance on admitting him. He figured it would be smart to take advantage of his dad's influence. Not just anyone could get the permits necessary for their son to live alone in a high-rise condo. His dad held some clout with the local officials. What was impossible for most citizens was still possible for Dr. Jay Griffin.

Li wasn't dumb. In fact, he had tested above the charts in the tests he had bothered to show up and take. He understood his father had survived, even thrived, during some pretty tumultuous times.

The year his father had graduated from high school was the year the country had begun its most tragic descent. It had grown economically desperate after years of recession, riots, terrorist attacks and an unfortunate barrage of natural disasters. Soon, even some of the most pessimistic commentators watched their outlandish prophecies become reality.

This is the way it was taught to him in school (though which one, Li couldn't remember)…

The previous government had long been held in disdain. In an unprecedented act, both the President and the Vice-President were assassinated on the same day. This tragedy threw the government into disarray. The country fell apart. After years of in-fighting, radical measures were taken to revolutionize the country from the ground up.

In 2044, a system was set up by the newly created Economic Crisis Containment Office. They now regulated every cent of every dollar. Actual paper and coin money had all been burned or melted down. Now, money was a chip embedded under the skin. People had to acquire a permit to spend money that hadn't been budgeted at their yearly budget consultation. Wages, taxes, spending, and even charities were all controlled by E.C.C.O. Composed of native authorities, they were held in check by foreign interests, mainly China, to whom E.C.C.O. owed a huge debt. They were allied together with the goals of paying off the country's debtors and of maintaining order.

This is what Li had been taught.

This is what he had observed.

Number one- though E.C.C.O. was voted in as a temporary band-aid, its power was growing. Li didn't believe they were ever going to give it up. Not without a fight.

Number two- his father was magnetically drawn to power. Li couldn't stand the way he kowtowed to the E.C.C.O. agents- but, at least he had his own apartment because of it.

It was now November 10, 2053. Half of Li's 18 years had been spent in Sector One, regulated by E.C.C.O. He wondered how much longer they would be in control. *Other people besides me must be sick of all their rules, right?*

Li bulleted back to his condo and grabbed his work bag with his scrubs, shoes, and toiletries in them. His dad was strict about everything, even the clothing policy; so it was best to abide by it, even though he wasn't going in for work, per se, but to meet his father off-hours for some as-yet-unknown reason.

He dreaded meeting him. His father criticized every single move he made and his expectations were exasperatingly high. Li was constantly reminded he should be eternally grateful the brilliant doctor had overseen every detail of his upbringing and he was lucky to have a father with the means to mold him into something worthwhile. And, not to be forgotten, he needed to remember one more thing - he hadn't lived up to his father's expectations.

Li had had schooling and training in a dozen different disciplines and he had excelled at all of them. The only thing he hadn't been able to master was his temper, which had been the sole reason for his being shuffled from school to school, year after year. Li had never stayed anywhere long enough to make a close friend, besides Carlos, the cleaning lady's son, and he'd never received any kind of approval from his father.

He'd grown to never expect it.

Thankfully, he only had to deal with 'The Devil' at rare times, even when working at the clinic. He had never been asked to come in so personally like this.

Come to think of it…his father usually ignored him at work, except when pointing out his mistakes. He was starting to feel a little queasy now.

When Li arrived at the Clinic, he entered through the back, went straight to the break room and found his locker. He changed into his fashion-deprived medical garb and inspected himself in the mirror. His deep brown, almond-shaped eyes, along with his tan skin, were a striking contrast to the stark whiteness of his shirt. His chin-length, jet black hair was now neatly collected in a band.

Li didn't look much like his father. This inspection in the mirror was as close as Li thought he would ever get to seeing who he really favored- his mother.

He knew little about her. His father had taken down any images of her and acted as though she had never existed. He had been told she left his father when Li was three years old. Li didn't blame her for leaving his father; he only wished she had taken him with her.

Li sauntered down the hallway, apprehension seeping from his stomach up into his throat. *This hallway never seemed so freakishly long before,* he thought. His footsteps echoed at a slow cadence.

He finally arrived at the door leading into his father's office. He touched the keypad on the wall to the right. After the loud beep, he heard his father's deep voice command, *"Jin!"*

His father had installed the Mandarin voice command system at the Clinic years ago. It gave him more control over who could come and go there. Jay Griffin had spent five years of his childhood in Beijing. He blatantly used his knowledge of Chinese to impress E.C.C.O. agents. His employees all had to learn just enough Pinyin (the Romanized phonetic expression of the Chinese language) to receive access to doors and company Coms, words like "enter" (*jin*), "lock" (*suo*), "answer" (*da fu*), and "end" (*wan bi*).

In Sector One, there was an undercurrent of resentment and prejudice towards China, though it was illegal to voice these feelings. Of course, in underground warehouses, Li found people to be very expressive.

The door opened for him automatically. *Don't show weakness, you wuss. He can smell fear.* He took a deep breath and walked in confidently. Li took a chance and grinned widely at his father.

"You beckoned?"

"Li, you haven't been reaching your full potential here at the clinic."

Li's large grin vanished.

"I've decided you will be filling a more specialized position from this day forward. I have assigned you to a special patient. You will be her nurse, her teacher, and her bodyguard. You will no longer work for the Clinic; you will work for me alone. Do you think you can handle that?"

The doctor ushered Li over to his holo-computer and used his strong, slender surgeon's hand to brush an image into the middle of the wall-sized screen. Ainsling Reid's freckled, smiling face appeared.

"Li, *wo de er zi* , my son, …meet Ainsling."

2 The Chick

Ainsling brushed her baby-fine, lengthy blonde hair in slow motion as she stared at her reflection in the mirror. *Now I have a chance to be normal, she thought.* Her heart was beating wildly with excitement and apprehension. She was in disbelief at her luck.

Because of her condition, she had been labeled "unproductive" by E.C.C.O. To be chosen for a special surgery, despite her lowly status, was... amazing. For the daughter of a single father, a factory laborer at that, it was near impossible! Now she would be leaving her lonely father and the familiarity of her insulated life.

Also, she had become addicted to a very unusual drug-knitting. She blamed Nurse Cheng for that. One day, she was walking through the atrium area of a hospital wing and noticed Nurse Cheng teaching another patient how to wrap a string around a needle, slide it down, create a loop, and then slide it off. She moved along loop by loop, magically creating fabric. Ainsling was fascinated by it, so she begged Nurse Cheng to teach her too. Now she was addicted! Scarves, blankets, hats, and even socks were in abundance in their tiny apartment, created by the skilled movement of her own two hands.

Because of her unproductive status, she had never personally purchased the yarn she knitted with now. It was all passed on to her through E.C.C.O.'s Distribution Network with the stipulation she made items out of it for charity. She never had the luxury of choosing green over blue, or wool over acrylic yarn. Whatever they sent her was what she had to work with. It forced her to be creative and frugal.

Ainsling had never gone shopping for anything. She wasn't given an implanted chip when she turned twelve, like everyone else. Nurse Cheng always commented that the many blankets, shawls, slippers and sweaters Ainsling had produced made the term "unproductive" an oxymoron, whatever that meant. Ainsling was more than happy to give away her knitted creations. Although, she did pity the poor person who received her first attempt at socks.

Now she would be going to receive a special operation and live at a new facility for patients like herself for a whole year! It was so incredibly amazing; she had been selected for the special surgery that would eliminate the seizures she now suffered from. Many had waited years, also suffering from the same type of seizures as Ainsling- seizures that weren't responsive to any of the dozen or so drugs used to regulate them.

She might have to make some sacrifices, but Ainsling felt confident it would all be worth it to be accepted into this world - to be normal.

In the last two weeks she hadn't knitted a stitch because of all the tests Dr. Sparks had been conducting on her to ensure that she was the perfect candidate for the case study. Some of the tests involved observing her during her seizures. After a seizure, Ainsling would sleep for hours. She spent the rest of her waking hours reading her favorite old books, trying to distract herself from worrying.

She was now 16. The few doctors she had seen had never been able to explain the reason for her resistance to medication.

Her father took her dispiriting condition to heart and blamed himself. Ainsling fought against his depressed attitude by adopting an overly optimistic one. His visits were always so brief that she didn't want any of the time wasted on sad thoughts. After losing her mother before Ainsling had even turned one year old, she was all he had left in this world. Ainsling was heartsick over being the reason for his sorrow. She wondered if he would be all right while she was gone. Sometimes he forgot to pick up his food rations and he often overslept and was late for work.

"Time to go, sweet girl!" Dr. Sparks' nurse knocked on the door before it opened and showed her round, smiling face.

"I'm ready," Ainsling said confidently, pushing all her anxieties about her father to the back of her mind, and allowed the nurse to take her bags. She sat in the wheelchair provided and allowed herself to be wheeled away towards her only chance for a normal future.

***

Li didn't sleep well. It was hard to decide which was stranger—his dad's behavior or his new job. He had accepted the new position, though it felt like he wasn't really being asked, but rather, *told* to accept it. That goofy girl's face kept popping up in his mind. She was just plain old weird.

His father hadn't given him any more information that night, explaining that the details were still being constructed into a program specific to her and that he would be receiving them the next day.

Oops, make that…today. Seriously, is that light actually the sun beaming through the window? Ugh.

He looked at the time on his Com. *Crap!* He had to get moving! He grabbed his stuff and ran out the door to the elevator. All the way to the clinic, he wondered about the enigmatic specifics for this unusual job. *Why the mystery?* All the other epilepsy candidates for surgery at the clinic didn't get this much attention. It was odd. *Why would he have to teach her? From what would she need to be guarded?* He had a million questions, yet his biggest concern was…

What would happen if he failed?

***

Li's father was in his office with about a dozen other doctors. Li deciphered they were doctors solely by the snarky air of superiority permeating the room. He cleared his throat obnoxiously to get his father's attention. The self-proclaimed "pioneer doctor" ignored him, finished his sentence and shook the other doctors' hands. They all filed out of the office. Li lifted an eyebrow and bided his time before his father acknowledged him.

"Did you sleep well, Li?" his father asked without looking his way.

"Not really, but I'm here, so tell me all about this Ainsling chick."

"She's not a chick, Li. In fact, the most familiar you are allowed to get with this girl is possibly 'buddy.' Got it, Romeo?"

Li rolled his eyes. His father really didn't know him at all.

"She's a goofy little kid. I think I can manage to restrain myself. Why don't you just go over the details of my new position, *boss?*"

Li's disrespectful tone did not go over well with his father. His countenance displayed inner turmoil. He was struggling to hold back his aggravation. A deep breath was necessary before he opened his mouth to address his impertinent son.

"Well, yes, I am your boss now and I demand a certain amount of respect from my employees, so please try to keep your adolescent angst to yourself from now on, Li. I know this isn't your dream job, but, since you have shown no interest in any other dream, you may as well accept this. Besides, we're both grown men. Let's work together like adults now."

Li's father threw one long arm around Li's shoulders and squeezed them forcefully. He then rapped him on the back

13

like a coach and said, "This is a golden opportunity! Medical research has been stifled for too long. Now that the country has some stability, I can forge ahead. This girl is in need of my help and I am in need of yours. Are you able to put aside all of our family issues and work together for the benefit of mankind?"

Li tried to keep a straight face. He had never heard his father say anything about the benefit of mankind before. He was pretty sure the only kind of man who would benefit here would be Dr. Griffin, neurosurgeon/egomaniac. But he couldn't think of any snappy comebacks right then, so he said eloquently,

"Uh, sure, whatever."

"Science holds the answer to questions no one has even thought to ask, Li. People are finally past defaulting to religion for answers. This is an opportunity for you to play a role, however small, in wanton exploration of the unexplored. The brain is the most mystifying part of the human animal. This girl's brain is essential to answering some of those unknown questions. You don't know how lucky you are to be *my* son, Li."

Li responded to this philosophical scientific soliloquy by staring blankly at his father's chiseled, tan face. His father must have interpreted his seemingly attentive look as encouragement because he then smiled as if satisfied and handed Li a computer pad.

"Well, that's enough chit-chatting. Here is your first week's schedule."

Li perused it, continuing to appear attentive, though he was still apprehensive and confused by this shroud of mystery. *What is my father really up to?*

"For the next few months, you will be residing in the adjoining room to Miss Reid, in order to give her the best care possible. So, please go home and pack your things and I will send someone to collect them in an hour."

"What?!? Living here at the clinic? A *few months?* You never said *anything* about-"

Dr. Griffin gave Li a fierce look that successfully stopped his outburst. He took an annoyed breath and bolted out of the office. On his way down the hall, he passed a petite blonde patient gliding along in a wheelchair, pushed by a nurse in pristine white garb. In his agitated state, he didn't really notice them, but the girl tugged on the nurse's sleeve behind her and whispered, "Who was that angry guy?"

She was answered by a tall, middle-aged man with a strong jaw and eagle-like eyebrows. When he smiled, his green eyes sparkled with gold flecks.

"That was my son. And you must be Ainsling. Am I right?"

Ainsling returned the doctor's smile and held out her hand. "Yes, I am. Why is your son so angry?"

"He's just having a rough day. Actually, he's a pretty amazing guy. Don't let him bother you."

He gave her a sparkling, confident smile. "I'm the head of this clinic, Dr. Griffin. It's very nice to meet you." He shook her outstretched hand and then patted it gently. Ainsling beamed at him with recognition, as if he was a celebrity and she was his biggest fan.

"Follow me, and I'll show you where you will be living for the next year." He winked at her and strode slowly towards her room as the nurse continued to push Ainsling along, following his lead.

"I really want to thank you, doctor! This is a dream come true for me. I know that you are the one that will cure me! I totally believe in you!"

Ainsling's voice was overcome with confidence. He smiled to himself and was inwardly amused by her childlike trust in him. Without turning around, he responded,

"I am very glad that you are here, Ainsling. This operation will change your life and I am honored to be a part of it. Ah, here's your room!"

Dr. Griffin led her into a huge room and opened the blinds to the windows. The sun shone in brightly and blinded them all momentarily. Everyone in the room blinked until their vision returned.

Ainsling stood up slowly from the wheelchair and walked over to her new doctor. She had tears in her eyes.

Her thin arms reached out to him and she gave him a strong hug. The doctor grasped her arms and gently pried them off. He leaned over and looked at her with his hypnotic gold-flecked eyes and said assuredly,

"Ainsling, I *will* cure you. After all, if nothing ever changed, there'd be no butterflies. Do you want to be a butterfly, Ainsling?"

She looked up at him and said with conviction,

"Yes, more than anything."

3 The Red String

Li threw his clothes haphazardly into a suitcase and beat himself up inside for not fighting his father over this whole "moving into the clinic" idea. *This was going to be torture!*

It was bad enough to have to work for his impossible-to-please father, now he had to give up his only tie to freedom, too. When he called Carlos and explained the horror that was his life to him, all Carlos could offer was, "That sucks, dude."

The doorbell rang and he reluctantly opened the door to find Mr. Reynolds, his dad's faithful lapdog, standing there with a business-like expression on his face.

He guessed this meant his moving crew was here. When Mr. Reynolds gestured behind him, his theory was proved correct. Ten men came in and emptied his condo in only thirty minutes. It had taken six hours to move everything into it himself; and now, in half an hour, it was as if he'd never lived there.

"I shall escort you back to the clinic now, Mr. Griffin. Your father suggested you meet with him in one hour to discuss your responsibilities. We should leave as soon as possible."

"Whatever."

There was a loud bang ahead of them. "Hey, be careful with my guitar, man!"

"All right, Reynolds, let's get moving. I wouldn't want to be late." Li knew his sarcasm was completely lost on Reynolds, but it made him feel better. He followed the benign man, dressed from head to toe in gray, out of his now former residence.

Li once again made his way to his father's office and reluctantly sat down at the massive desk. His father was annoyingly chipper as he explained Li's new job responsibilities. He tried his best to ignore his disturbing cheerfulness. His father explained to him that this patient, the little blonde girl, would be undergoing a special brain surgery in eight weeks. The goal until then would be to keep her healthy and prepare her for the "productive" life she would lead after the device was installed. His job consisted of escorting her to appointments, tutoring her in her academic studies, and keeping her company.

It sounded a lot like babysitting. Of course, being trained as a medical assistant, he would also be required to record her vital statistics regularly. Since she suffered from unpredictable tonic clonic seizures, he would need to be on constant alert and follow the standard medical rules in the event of a seizure. She was not allowed to do anything dangerous, such as strenuous exercise, and she absolutely could not leave the clinic.

"Would you like to meet her while your things are being unpacked?"

Li didn't have any defendable reason to delay it, so he solemnly nodded his head yes. His father stood up and offered his hand to Li. He just stared at it for a few seconds, but then awkwardly shook the man's slender, strong hand. After years of minimal face-to-face interaction, this touchy-feely stuff was alien to him. He was more comfortable pulling people into headlocks than he was shaking his own father's hand.

"I trust you will not let me down, Li. I am proud to have you on my team. You know, I used to work side-by-side with my father, but that was a long time ago. I hope you learn much from this experience, son. Let's go!"

"Yes, sir," Li heard himself mutter. He was still wandering in alien territory. His father never talked about family, and certainly never expressed any interest in working side-by-side with Li before.

He followed him like a compliant employee to meet the new patient, wondering how much more awkward this was going to get.

Dr. Griffin held his hand over the security pad and announced himself. A sweet, childlike voice sang out, "You may enter, Dr. Griffin! *Jin!*"

They entered the hospital room together, Li following his father cautiously. The room was bathed in sunlight and hardly looked like a typical hospital room. It was bright and cheerful and interspersed haphazardly with handmade rag rugs, crocheted blankets, and boxes overflowing with clothing, books, and yarn. Li scanned the room through the eccentric rainbows of color for the girl they were supposed to be there to see. Finally, he found her. She was sitting on the floor reading a tattered old book. He tried to glimpse the title and got as far as "Harry Po-"

"I see you have been learning our specialized voice-command entry system, Ainsling. I'm impressed. Have you made yourself at home? I hope you don't mind if I introduce you to your personal aide now," his father addressed the petite waif-like girl.

The small girl's face lit up at the site of Dr. Griffin.

"Oh, yes, thank you for allowing me to bring all my things!" She clasped her hands in front of her face, then looked behind Dr. Griffin and saw Li.

"Hey, isn't he the angry boy? Your...your son, right?"

Li raised his eyebrows and looked curiously back and forth between his father and the girl.

"Yes, it is. May I introduce you? Ainsling, this is Li. Li, this is Ainsling."

Ainsling jumped to her feet quickly and directed her glaring, unpretentious smile up at Li, who was a good foot taller than her. Embarrassed, he caught himself just before involuntarily smiling back. She was so small and immature! He knew intellectually that it was now his job to take care of her, but something inside of him rose up like a lost ballon and, though it was a small feeling, it was there nonetheless. He felt like he *wanted* to take care of her. He tried to ignore it: it was another one of those alien feelings, just as annoying as his father's newfound "affection" for him.

He couldn't deny that this strange girl had singlehandedly transformed this whole room. The normally drab cubicle-like confines were significantly warmer and brighter. Homey, even. He had never seen anything like it. It was uncanny. *Yep, definitely an alien,* he thought.

Out loud, to the alien's face, he said, "The angry boy, huh? Look, I've been informed that I have the pleasure of being your warden. I'd prefer to be called something other than 'angry boy,' though; but, whatever."

Li's sarcasm was as thick as he could manage in front of his father. She seemed to be oblivious to it, though he doubted his father hadn't noticed. He ignored him, though. The alien girl twirled a section of her blonde hair around her finger and considered him a minute. He began to feel uncomfortable under her gaze.

"Hmmm…well, Li, nicknames are special things. I'll have to observe you for a while and see what works. 'Bubba?' 'Li-Man?' 'Speedy?' 'Teach?' Your father told me that you're amazing. Oooo…*The Amazing Li!*"

Her words were as playful as her eyes. This girl spoke as

if she were both a wise old lady and a simple child morphed into one person.

She encouraged this impression when she suddenly bounced across the room like a toddler, searched through a cardboard box of soft, brightly colored wool, and victoriously lifted up a ball of red yarn. She unwound 8 inches of it and cut it with a small pair of scissors.

Li followed her quizzically with his dark eyes as she bounced back across the room. When she returned to him, she grabbed his right hand. She laid the string across his palm gently, as if laying down a sleeping baby.

"Have you ever heard of the red string of destiny?" she asked a little shyly. Her cheeks flushed a light pink and her freckles darkened.

"No," Li replied flatly.

"Well, maybe if you show me that you are amazing, as I've been informed you are, I'll tell you all about it. For now, consider it a good luck present." She winked and gave him a lop-sided goofy grin.

This girl's brain could definitely use some surgery, thought Li. But he managed to keep his mouth shut. This girl was truly odd. He glanced at the scrap of yarn in his hand. *Yeah, right- good luck.*

He had almost forgotten that his father was there. His baritone voice interrupted the awkward silence.

"Well, you two, today's schedule is open. Tomorrow we will begin your school curriculum and start tutoring. Ainsling, Li will also be your tutor. This way you will have a head start on all the schooling you'll need to catch up on when you change your status to a "productive" member of society after the surgery. In addition, every day at 6 p.m., Li will escort you to my office. We will be discussing your surgery and its life-altering effects in detail."

He could barely contain himself as he declared next, "This is an exciting time!"

Dr. Griffin gazed back and forth between Ainsling and Li. Ainsling beamed back at him while Li grimaced, working hard to avoid his father's eyes.

"Li, I suggest you get your room organized and prepare for tomorrow's lessons. Please follow the curriculum provided. We'll leave you alone now, Ainsling. Sleep well tonight! Tomorrow is when it all begins!"

He nodded at Li and motioned for him to precede him out of Ainsling's room. As he passed Ainsling, Li held up the red string and said to her,

"Uh, thanks for the present. See you tomorrow." He crumpled it up and stuffed it into his pocket so he could throw it out later.

Ainsling involuntarily blushed. After they exited the room, she fell back on her heavily blanketed bed. She couldn't believe her luck- a cure and a friend.

4 The Lessons

Ellen answered her Com. It was midnight. Only one person would be calling her at this hour.

"Hello," she whispered. There was silence on the other end. "Any news?" she asked urgently.

"The girl is at Griffin's clinic now. Her surgery is scheduled in eight weeks."

"I will be waiting for instructions."

"They will be given. I thank you on behalf of the Guardian."

"It is my honor."

Ellen took a deep breath and closed her eyes. It was hard to trust in someone she'd never seen, but she had made a vow to obey him, so she must do her best. She reached out to pet her fat, lazy cat, Whiskers. He purred back his thanks. At the moment, Ellen envied Whiskers' ability to sleep soundly- he had no cares, no worries, no responsibilities to interrupt his dreams.

***

Ainsling's door beeped and a young male voice sounded through the intercom, "Are you awake? It's Li Griffin."

She had been awake for almost two hours, before the sun had even risen. It was hard to contain her excitement. She remained in awe of this life-changing opportunity. Waiting eight weeks for her surgery was going to be excruciating!

At that second she decided to embark on a personal mission to needle out everything she could discover about her new tutor. *That's what friends do, right?* It might keep her mind busy enough to wait through the next eight weeks without going absolutely crazy.

"Yes, uh, *Jin!*"

At Ainsling's command, the door opened for Li, so he sauntered in. He hoped she was up to all the work ahead. *Ugh, I'll never have any time for myself!* Sighing, he imagined his guitar languishing under his bed and gathering dust.

Even eight weeks was hardly enough time to learn all the material his father had given to him to teach her. *There will be no time for fun and games, that's for sure,* thought Li.

"How-"

"Are-"

They both began talking at the same time. Ainsling laughed giddily and apologized, "Sorry, you first!"

"I was just going to ask if you are a good student," Li frowned as he set up the computer on the desk provided in her room. He grudgingly removed a box of gaudy pink yarn from the desk and dropped it harshly onto the floor. *There's yarn everywhere,* he thought, annoyed. The room was eclectic and colorful, but it was also distracting and messy. *How could anyone concentrate in a room like this?*

"Oh, I'm mostly self-taught. I took the basic elementary courses from the E.C.C.O. education network, but I reached the standard limit for people like me when I was eleven. So since then, I just read!"

Her hand caressed a tattered book beside her on the bed where she was sitting.

"What I really like are the actual paper books- you know, the old-fashioned kind? There's something special about holding the words in your hands, hearing the turning of the pages. Plus, they give away old paper books, which is awesome since my father's status doesn't allow him to budget money for technology. We don't have a Com for digital books, of course."

She paused in her rambling.

"My father is a factory worker," she explained.

"Oh," Li responded.

Li was embarrassed for her. Factories were, in actuality, forced labor facilities. Those who worked there included the formerly unemployed, former "productive" welfare recipients and once petty criminals pardoned early from the overcrowded prison systems.

The factories were run much like prisons, with small dormitory-like apartments provided for each worker and strict housing rules. The workers' incomes were low, and, like everyone's, strictly regulated by E.C.C.O. They didn't have a lot left for luxuries. Even if her father hadn't been a criminal (though Li wasn't really interested in whether he was or not), he lived like one. Li felt a slight pang of sympathy, which he tried to ignore.

"What were you going to say?" he asked, trying to change the subject. He wanted to shake the awkwardness in the air.

"Say? Oh- before? Right! I was going to ask you how old you are. You seem too young to work here!"

"I'm eighteen!" he said haughtily. "I was a medical assistant with my own apartment and a *life* before you came along!"

She recoiled slightly at his heated response. He tried to be less abrasive. "I took a few pre-med courses at boarding school because my father forced me to. When I refused to go to college this year, my father punished me by making me work here until I decide to follow in his great footsteps and major in medicine or science, neither of which interests me. Any other questions?"

"Oh I have lots of questions! Why were you angry the other day in the hallway? What's it like having a father who's a genius? What's your mother like? Do you have any brothers or sisters? What's your-"

"Whoa- slow down! Maybe you shouldn't ask questions you might not like the answers to."

"What won't I like?"

Ainsling's doe-eyed expression met his agitated one.

"Well, number one- the reason I was angry is none of your business! Number two- having a genius doctor for a father is a major pain! Number three- my mother left me when I was little and I have no siblings, it's just me. Was that all?"

"Um, yes. Sorry, Li."

Ainsling concentrated her gaze towards the floor and fell silent. Li felt a little guilty, but he figured she could use a healthy dose of reality. She was way too cheerful! It was annoying.

"Look, let's start the lesson, now. Okay?"

"Sure!" Ainsling perked up and sat in the chair at the desk while Li pulled up the first file on the holo-computer and began the tutoring session. It was two hours before he announced they should take a break.

Ainsling got up and stretched. She picked up a box with a knitted blanket in progress lying in it. She pulled out the instructions and found her place. The repetitious movements were soothing to her.

Li was busy closing down the program. When he was finished, he turned around and discovered her knitting in earnest, the needles producing light clicking sounds.

Fifteen minutes went by before Ainsling felt the weight of his eyes studying her. She set down her needles and looked up at his serious face.

"Should I teach *you* something now?" she asked playfully.

"What? Knitting? Please!" He rolled his eyes.

"Oh, yeah, you probably couldn't do it anyway," she said, prodding at his ego.

"Fine- if it'll get you to be quiet and stop asking me annoying questions- I'll do it. Once."

Ainsling smiled mischievously to herself.

***

Dr. Griffin watched the screen in front of him with great interest. He was entertained by the interaction of the two main characters. It was a pleasant distraction from his work at the moment.

Eight weeks should be enough time, he thought. He sipped his coffee and made some notes on his Com. He had been making adjustments to his invention. The prototype needed to be specifically programmed to Ainsling Reid's brain. All the scans and tests would help him to achieve this. He was confident he would succeed this time. He *must* succeed.

Epilepsy research had been halted in the country except for a select few facilities until E.C.C.O. had been established. He had no real competition, and the FDA was now defunct; so, FDA approval was no longer a roadblock, as it had been to researchers like his father, who had fled the U.S. to work in China after coming under the FDA's scrutiny.

The device he had invented was loosely based off former devices once used to treat and study seizures in the early 2000's. One such device was called a vagus nerve stimulator and was implanted in the chest. It could block specific brain impulses that tell the body to seize. Another similar device was surgically implanted in a hollowed out section of the skull, with electrical leads placed through the parts of the brain which were identified by the patient's neurosurgeon as the "seizure focus." This device was the most similar to his invention.

He had already determined Ainsling's seizure focus. That was easy. The harder part concerned the second tier of functions of the device, the part his father had begun before he fled the country for Beijing, to continue without the human-rights-heavy FDA interference. When his father died unexpectedly, Jay Griffin made an oath to himself to undertake his pet project in secret in his homeland.

The serum involved had worked successfully in all the lab animals, yet all his human subjects so far had failed. Failure meant death.

The explanations were varied, but he was confident he had now eliminated all the negative variables. It had taken him nearly 20 years to perfect the serum. He was highly aware that the combination of these two concepts in this singular device would forever cement his name in scientific history.

5 The Good Boy

Ainsling entered Dr. Griffin's office everyday at exactly 6 p.m. for the next four weeks. Li insisted she be on time, but he didn't go in with her. The meetings consisted of more scans and lots of discussion. Her doctor took great pains in attempting to explain to her how her condition was unique. He explained the details of her brain scan results, the surgical procedure itself, and some vague details of the device he had invented. It was overwhelmingly complicated and boring. She tried to be polite and nod at all the appropriate times. It was plain to her that the doctor was by far the smartest person she had ever met.

As the weeks passed, she noticed a few interesting quirks that both Dr. Griffin and Li shared, which made her laugh. Whenever they both talked about something they knew a lot about, they got very excited and talked faster and faster, so fast she could barely understand their words. For Dr. Griffin, this usually occurred when he discussed the new device. For Li, it was music and mathematics. Also, they both habitually rubbed the back of their neck with their left hand. They both had slender, long fingers. She noticed how they shared the same nose and how their eyes always twinkled when they smiled.

Today Ainsling's mind wandered back to the picture of Li's long fingers dexterously maneuvering wooden needles and white yarn. She smiled to herself. He had become quite proficient. *It must be because he is smart, also like his father.* Li had recently remarked to her how some of her knitting patterns involved complex algebra skills and must have attributed to her surprisingly high math scores. She took this as a compliment; and, since Li rarely said anything positive, it was. Dr. Griffin noticed her dreamy look and smiled knowingly, as if he knew exactly what she was dreaming about.

That evening, Li met her back at her suite. She couldn't help giggling at the sight of him.

"You are too damn happy!" he scolded. "What could you possibly be laughing about? Is there a clown behind me?" He enjoyed reprimanding her for her many quirks. Teasing her made his job... fun.

"It's a secret." At this response, he rubbed his neck in frustration, which made her giggle even harder.

"Like your red string theory?"

"It's not a 'red string theory', silly. It's 'the red string of destiny.'"

"Whatever. Are you ever going to tell me what it is?" He actually sounded curious now instead of arrogant. Without his knowledge or approval, his arrogance was slowly but surely being eroded by her exuberant optimism.

"Not yet! I'm not fully convinced you're really as amazing as your father said you were. Besides, I'm too busy trying to think of a nickname for you."

"Li *is* my nickname. It's short for 'Liang.'" He didn't tell too many people this. As he had learned at the clubs, it didn't pay to flaunt his ancestry. Some people had serious issues with it, at least those who resented the current economic situation. As if it was *his* fault the country had to pay China back. Besides, he'd never even been to China!

"What does it mean?" Ainsling was curious. "Do you know?"

"Yes, I do." He paused, as if considering whether or not to continue. After thinking it over a bit, he decided to proceed.

"The only thing my father kept of my mom's was *me*. He didn't name me though- she did. For some crazy reason, she decided to give me a traditional Chinese name. 'Liang' means bright or good. Anyway, my father has never addressed me by my given name, so I've always gone by 'Li.'" He avoided her eyes. "I've never told this to anyone before. No one ever asks."

"Well, thanks for telling me. I feel special now." She meant it sincerely.

"It's cool - *'Li-ang,'*" Ainsling pronounced the name slowly. "She called you 'good.'" Ainsling's eyes got misty.

"She didn't know me," Li muttered. He poked her side playfully with his elbow, "What about you? What does your name mean?"

"It means 'dream.' My papa told me they decided on that name because I was a dream come true." Ainsling was a bit embarrassed, but also pleased.

Li continued to ask her questions.

"What's your mom like? Crazy, like you?"

"Well, she died in an accident when I was a baby, but papa says she was as beautiful as a sunset and as sweet as candy." Li had never seen her look so sad before. It was odd- odder than her cheesy, bubbly look.

Ainsling and Li's hands were so close they were almost touching. As a gesture of sympathy, Li placed his hand lightly on Ainsling's. He remarked on how different in size their hands were. But then Li didn't pull his hand back. She curled her small fingers around his long, slender hand.

"I guess we actually have something in common," he remarked. "Mysterious mothers. My mom left me when I was 3. I barely remember her. I'll never forgive her for it. She may as well be dead." Li's face was full of bitterness. He glanced at Ainsling and noticed she still had that out-of-place sad expression. It bothered him. He couldn't take it anymore. He pulled her up.

"Let's stop talking about our parents. I'm hungry. Let's get some ice cream!" He smiled freely at Ainsling and her face brightened.

Li ran towards the dining hall and Ainsling giggled, then ran after him. It was past regular working hours, so they served themselves. The clinic was small and had a limited staff. Li felt like he was back at boarding school, sneaking around after curfew.

Ainsling's mind kept circulating back to their mutually sad beginnings. *'The sun rises and the rain falls on both the good and the bad'*, her father once told her. Somehow, this adage helped her. It seemed to imply, at the very least, that it wasn't their fault.

They opened the freezer and picked out the flavors they liked best and sat down at a small table with some spoons. They talked for a while about trivial things, like favorite foods and music they liked. Ainsling was impressed with Li's knowledge of music. He told her that he played the acoustic guitar and used to be in a band at his former school. Ainsling had never played any instrument before, so she couldn't help but admire him for it. He promised to teach her some chords on his guitar the next day if they got through all of tomorrow's scheduled material.

"I'm curious about something," she told him.

"About what?"

"Well, I don't mean to pry, but, I just don't understand why you won't go to college and become a doctor like your father. I mean, you're smart, you're capable and you're economically able. I would give anything to be you!"

Li knew it would be hard to explain to her why he didn't want to become a doctor. For the first time, he was a little ashamed of the way he'd lived his life. She would also never believe he was even capable of getting into a fight. He knew she had a warped view of him. She saw things in him that he wasn't.

"I guess I feel like I need to follow my own path. I don't want to do something because my father tells me to. I want to do it because it's *my* choice. Don't you want to be free to decide your future, too?"

"Don't let an E.C.C.O. agent hear you say that! 'Seek freedom and become captive to your desires', remember? We finished that lesson yesterday. That's why the people led all those riots and even murdered the President. Freedom is very dangerous," she replied fearfully.

"Maybe. But what if it's worth it? Just think- after your surgery, you will be free to knit things for yourself. You can pick the color, the fiber, everything. Doesn't that make you happy?"

"Yeah, it does!" She smiled wide and he laughed.

Ainsling was so thankful she met Li. She was almost confident she could share the red string story with him now. The only thing holding her back was the fear he wouldn't believe in it. If he didn't believe it, well, then, she might lose the best friend she had ever had. She didn't know what she would do if he laughed at her.

Suddenly Ainsling's head began to ache. She informed Li and he put his hand on her forehead to quickly check her temperature. As soon as he touched her, he felt her body begin to seize.

Her body shook erratically. He cradled her head in his hands and slowly brought her down to the floor. He turned her head to the side. She convulsed uncontrollably, her limbs systematically jerking about. He held her head on his lap until it had completely passed, about ten minutes later.

Surprisingly, she then opened her eyes and gave him a weak smile. She whispered, "Good boy."

Then she passed out.

Li carried her limp, small frame back to her room and made Ainsling comfortable in her bed. He hooked her up to the I.V. drip. She had sweat beads on her forehead, so he took a wet towel and wiped it away. Sitting beside her, he checked his Com for the time. That's when he noticed his own heartbeat throbbing loudly in his ears. Yet, Ainsling's breathing was slow and her pulse was back to normal. He made himself match her breathing pattern.

Li wrapped himself up in one of her many blankets, knitted from random leftover yarn. He tried to relax. It was over. She was all right now.

She looked so peaceful lying there. Li leaned in and studied her face. He counted her freckles- sixteen. As many freckles as years she had lived. The gravity of her situation weighed on him. He sincerely hoped she would indeed be healed soon. He came to realize he honestly cared about this strange person. And he liked that feeling.

Li fell asleep in the chair beside Ainsling, wrapped in her woolen handiwork. He woke to the sound of the door beeping. He looked over at Ainsling. She was still asleep. Her pulse and heart rate were normal. He called out, "*Jin!*"

His father entered. He took large strides over to Li. Li opened his mouth to talk, but before he even formed a syllable, his father's palm struck his left cheek. Li was startled, then angry.

"When were you going to tell me that she had a seizure?" Dr. Griffin yelled at him.

"She's fine now! I never left her! Wait- how did you know?" Li looked at his father accusingly.

"That is not the point! The point is that *I'm* her doctor, not you! You are relieved of duty. I'll find someone better to take care of her now. You can go out and do whatever it is you do with your free time! I'll let you know when- or if- you can come back!"

Li's anger grew. Before he stormed out of the room, he took one more look at Ainsling's sleeping face. Then his anger turned in towards himself. Of course he should have told his father about the seizure! He knew what his father was like. Now he was being sacked and there was no way his father would give him another chance!

Li left the clinic and rode the Metro Bullet aimlessly for hours before he realized that he had accidentally taken the motley colored blanket with him. It made him mad all over again. Why hadn't he taken a minute and report to his father after Ainsling's seizure?

Ainsling. Poor Ainsling. During the seizure, he had been singularly focused on her. He had only thought about her welfare, not his job security. He wondered what his father would tell her. All the thoughts swirling around in his brain started to make his head throb. Thankfully, they were sidetracked when someone behind him on the Metro tapped him on the shoulder.

"Where did you get this blanket?" an older woman asked with a shocked tone in her voice. He wondered if she thought he had stolen it. Imagining how strange he looked with a loudly colored blanket wrapped around him, he was embarrassed.

"What? This? My friend made it." He hesitated before the word 'friend,' but decided there was no better word. To his surprise, the lady suddenly smiled wide.

"I think we have the same friend," she said and pulled out her scarf to full length. It was a variation on a similar kaleidoscope of yarns constructed in the same mitered squares pattern. They looked like fraternal samples of the same patchwork quilt.

The gentle-faced woman invited Li to go to a coffee shop with her. He felt a little strange about it, but this woman knew Ainsling! It would be interesting to talk with someone who knew her, too. So he followed her to a small café that was crowded with customers. Luckily, they found an empty table and sat down amidst the low rumble of many voices talking around them.

"This is a weird coincidence. How do you know Ainsling?"

"I was the one who taught her how to knit that blanket. My name is Ellen. Ainsling practically grew up at the hospital I work at. Unfortunately, there was little we could do for her. She left us about six weeks ago to undergo tests for a surgical opportunity. Did you get elected for surgery as well?"

The woman's face was caring. He could imagine her as a nurse. Nurses came in two varieties- compassionate or cruel. She was definitely in the compassionate camp.

"No, I'm not a patient. I'm her personal aide. Well, I was." He took a sip of warm coffee to distract him from his feelings of regret.

"You were? What happened? Is Ainsling all right?" The woman looked panicked.

"Oh, don't worry! Ainsling is fine! I was fired. I… made a mistake."

The woman sighed in relief and then studied Li's face.

"You care about her, don't you?" she asked. "It's because she's Ainsling. You can't know her and not like her. She's quite unique, huh?" Her smile reached into her eyes as she mentioned her former patient and friend.

"That's true. She's one of a kind."

Li took another sip of coffee and started to feel the caffeine surge through his veins. He told Ellen some of the funny things Ainsling had done or said and she laughed. She shared a few stories of her own. He even confessed to her that Ainsling had taught him to knit. Before they knew it, two hours had passed. It was so refreshing to relax and be distracted from his problems.

"Did she ever tell you about the red string of destiny?" Li asked her, feeling incredibly dorky as the word "destiny" rolled out of his mouth awkwardly.

"I'm not sure, but it sounds like something Ainsling would like. You know, most of the epilepsy patients I've worked with struggle with depression, but not Ainsling. She's special. I think it's because of her father. Plus, she reads so many stories! She is looking for something to believe in. I suppose it's one of the reasons she is so optimistic," Li looked downcast. She had easily believed in him too. And he had let her down. His companion noticed his sudden change of countenance. The woman reached out, touched his arm, and said compassionately, "Let me take you somewhere, if you have time. It's close by!"

Li followed the woman for a few blocks and found himself in an old store that had walls loaded with displays of yarn. It was spilling out from every crevice. The nurse led him over to a whole wall dedicated to the color red. Fuzzy rouge red mohair, shiny ruby silk, and warm, russet red wool were waiting to be touched and knitted into something special. Ellen smiled at his eyes widening, taking it all in.

"Look, Li. It's a whole wall of 'destiny' red! Let me buy one for you. I have a little left in my budget," she said, glancing at her hand which contained her chip.

She helped him pick out a soft cotton and wool blend. He'd never purchased yarn before, so he was glad she was there. As far as the shop keeper knew, he could've been her son. They had the same eyes and skin. She was probably his mother's age.

He recalled his conversation last night with Ainsling. He really missed her, though he couldn't explain why. Seriously, she was the weirdest person he had ever known.

When they were parting, the woman gave Li a quick hug, which left him feeling strange. He supposed he wouldn't have felt that way if he had a mother who'd hugged him before. She told him how wonderful it had been to meet him and hear about Ainsling. She gave him his bag from the shop.

"Be strong, Li. Things have a way of working out in the end." She gave him a compassionate look and winked.

Li watched her walk towards the Metro station. *Now where should I go?* He wondered. He started to take a tentative step forward. A small prick on the back of his neck was the last thing he remembered.

6 The Cure

Ainsling woke up confused and terribly thirsty. Someone handed her a cup of water and she drank it greedily. She began to feel more normal and looked over at her visitor. It was Dr. Griffin.

"I heard you had an eventful evening."

"Oh, well, I had a seizure, I guess. All I remember is eating ice cream and-"

She stopped herself from finishing her thought out loud. The memory of Li's face and the warm feel of his hands cradling her head produced a feeling of comfort and safety that overwhelmed her. She wanted to keep this memory to herself. It was hers.

The doctor grimaced and picked up the conversation.

"Well, it appears that you have recovered well. Are you ready for some good news? We are going to move up your surgery. How does *tomorrow* sound?"

"Really? Are you sure? Tomorrow works for me! I can't wait to tell Li!"

Dr. Griffin's forced merriment faded as he thought about how to respond next.

"I had to send Li on a personal errand, so he will be away for a few days. I will be looking in on you from time to time today. You need to rest. Are you hungry?"

"A little." She was also a little sad. *Li wouldn't be around?*

"Well, you may have liquids until noon and then you will have to fast in order to be prepped for surgery in the morning. I am very excited for you, Ainsling!" He stood up and beamed at her with his gold flecked eyes again.

He rubbed the back of his neck with his left hand, spurning Ainsling's longing for Li's presence even more. She knew her father would not be able to come because of his job. She was on her own.

***

Dr. Griffin was in his office. His Com rang out and he saw the caller's name appear. He said confidently, *"Da fu!"*

"Is everything in order, Dr. Griffin? You will call us immediately after the patient presents; is that understood?" the caller spoke curtly, demanding an answer. Yet, Griffin was not easily intimidated.

"Don't worry; I will notify you, as requested. Just remember that we are not equals in this world-changing development. I am not taking orders. This is my accomplishment. I am the only doctor on this planet capable of attaining this medical miracle. I have worked hard for this. Don't presume to bully me."

"Don't act like you are self-funded! You may be the only doctor capable of this today, but we are very patient. Be sure all the security measures are in place, doctor. Good bye."

The phone call annoyed the doctor, but he was not deterred. He verified his plans, checked on the device, and downed a glass of champagne. He had succeeded in everything thus far. The patient was perfectly flawed. The theory was absolutely genius. The timing was impeccable.

He was pleased that he had left his previous position. His former supervisor would never have allowed him to advance as far as he had by working on his own, with unbridled freedom.

The scientific community failed him. He had worked harder than any of his peers. Then, out of jealousy, he was accused of violating human rights. They fired him and branded him "immoral," as they had his father years before. No one could accept the fact that hard sacrifices must be made for significant scientific progress. In time, though, the world would revere him for his amazing contribution to science as it had applauded those who came before him.

There were already many revered neuroscientists throughout history. Ivan Pavlov became famous for his study of behavior modification. He not only influenced science, but popular culture as well. People threw around the phrase "Pavlov's dog" without even understanding the important contribution to neuroscience that had been made by Ivan Pavlov's research.

Dr. Ben Carson made medical history by being the first surgeon to successfully separate conjoined twins, perilously linked by their heads. This surgical prodigy also made his mark in the field of epilepsy when he performed a hemispherectomy. Young children suffering from uncontrollable seizures were cured, though the risk of mental retardation was high. Hemispherectomy is a procedure which involves removing one half of the brain. This difficult procedure spurred the further study of epilepsy and seizures, to which Griffin was personally grateful to Dr. Carson for.

Sam Harris and David Eagleman used their knowledge of neuroscience in writing books. Sam Harris delved into philosophy, becoming an anti-religion icon. Both he and Mr. Eagleman, a Guggenheim Fellow and expert on time perception and synesthesia, became New York Times bestselling authors. Neuroscience was once a media darling. Griffin himself, as a young man, had been thoroughly enamored by its motley charms. He didn't need much parental encouragement to follow in his father's steps as a neuroscientist. It was what he always wanted to become.

Ben Carson, Sam Harris, David Eagleman, Ivan Pavlov... they were mere stepping stones. Amateurs. Dr. Jay Griffin would outdo them all.

***

The morning of the surgery, Ainsling awoke and decided she should write a note for her father and for Li. There was always the possibility... Anyway, it was just a good idea. She found one of her notebooks and began to write. Just as she finished, her door beeped.

"*Jin!*"

Ainsling reflected on how wonderful her life would be when she was free from her seizures. She could live like everyone else. She would be worth something. Her father could stop being sad. The look of hopelessness she often saw in his eyes would disappear.

Dr. Griffin and a team of medical staff in sea-green garb entered. He was smiling brightly, causing his eyes to practically glow.

"Ready?"

"Ready!"

***

The surgical facility was equipped with the latest technology, even some that had been created specifically for this procedure. Dr. Griffin had picked his assistants very carefully. They had all been waiting for this day in secret. No one else was allowed in the clinic today except this group of thirteen.

The procedure lasted eight hours. He never stopped to rest or to eat. As he closed up, he admired his work. He had done it! She had survived the surgery. The device, which would stop her seizures and also make scientific history, was intricately implanted in her brain.

They went into the sterile room and Dr. Griffin removed his gloves. He rubbed the back of his neck. The rest of his team congratulated him, taking turns shaking his hand.

He smiled back at them as he put on an oxygen mask and pulled out an aluminum cylinder. Before any of them noticed, he pushed the plunger and dispersed a substance into the air and waited for the whole team to succumb to the strong poison. They had done their jobs. He couldn't let them live. That would be foolish. He refused to allow this knowledge to be shared and left vulnerable to replication.

After the air cleared, he opened the door and wheeled an unconscious Ainsling into an ambulance. He clicked the belts across her small body. The ambulance drove out of the city and, a few hours later, Griffin set off the explosions he had set up beforehand with his Com. The evidence and any possibility of recreation by anyone other than himself were completely destroyed.

Dr. Griffin made two calls before the one which destroyed his Clinic. The first was to Mr. Reynolds. The second was to the caller from the night before.

"So, does it work?"

"There is no way to test it until she has awoken."

"When will that be?"

"Soon. Very soon. Have patience."

***

The sun hadn't risen yet, but Connor Reid was awake. He was scheduled for the early shift this week. He sipped his coffee and listened to the radio. It was broadcasting the daily E.C.C.O. news report. A polite knock rang out from the hollow wood door near the kitchenette. It echoed softly across his small two room apartment. He'd never had a visitor this early. Actually, until Ainsling had been chosen out of the blue for that surgery, he'd never even had a visitor! He lowered the volume on the radio, since turning it off was illegal, and got up.

He opened the door to find a well-dressed man in a pressed grey suit. He recognized him immediately. It was the same man who had come to tell them about Ainsling's random selection for surgery.

"Mr. Reynolds, was it? What can I do for you?"

Mr. Reynolds' face was expressionless. "May I come in, Mr. Reid?"

Connor opened the door slightly wider and made room for him to enter the small apartment.

"How's my girl? It's just a few more weeks till the surgery, right?" He suddenly found himself quite nervous in front of this finely dressed man.

"Well, her surgery was moved up. She had had another seizure and the doctor decided it was best to move forward. Unfortunately, the surgery did not go as planned." He paused.

"Her body was too weak to survive the long surgery, Mr. Reid. I'm afraid she succumbed."

"Succumbed?"

"She died, sir."

Connor stared at the cot Ainsling once slept on. He was in shock. He knew he shouldn't have let her go! But she begged and begged. He didn't have the heart to say no. Now she was gone. His precious dream had died.

"I have brought her things to you. On the top of this box is a letter she wrote to you right before her surgery. I am sincerely sorry, Mr. Reid."

Mr. Reynolds stood and walked out to the hall. He picked up a box and carried it into the little apartment. As he set it down, it made a hollow thump that echoed in the tiny dwelling. Connor Reid didn't stir. He had laid his head down on the table and was sobbing quietly. Reynolds left the apartment in silence. He had done what he came to do.

As he was walking out of the workers' housing project, he pulled out his Com. He sent the message.

"Mission accomplished."

7 The Loss

"Look, Preach- I don't want to hear another word about it! We voted, and that's that! He's perfectly fine."

"I understand how you feel, Dave. It *was* a little extreme, but the message said he was in danger and that we needed to act now. Oh, look! I think he's waking up!"

Li's head ached. His eyelids were heavy, but the sound of loud voices helped wake him from his sleep. He couldn't make out anything at first, only fuzzy shapes. Then the shapes clarified and he found himself looking up at three strikingly dissimilar faces, the sources of the voices he'd just heard. One was a woman with chocolate brown skin and strong cheekbones. The next, to her right, was a gray-haired man with bright blue eyes behind his glasses and worry lines on his forehead. The last was one he recognized- the nurse from the Metro, Ellen.

"What's going on? Where am I?"

Li attempted to sit up and was helped by one of the strangers. He felt dizzy and a little nauseous. His neck was sore and he was unaware of how much time had passed since he had been standing with Ellen at the Metro.

"I'm sorry, Li. The group decided together to bring you here this way. To be honest, I voted against it! Are you feeling okay?" The grandfatherly man with short grey hair tried to smile through his concern.

"Uh, I'm okay, I guess. My stomach hurts a little. You didn't answer my questions." His head started to clear. The woman he'd never met stood up and held her hand out and firmly pulled him to his feet.

"Plenty of time for questions after supper, young man." She had a strong arm and a provincial accent. She must've lived in the city all her life.

"By the way, my name is Aaliyah. This is Dave, our resident pastor, and this is our best nurse, Ellen. Let's get you some food and then we can talk some more."

Li was too confused to argue, so he just grimaced. He got to his feet and slowly followed after the unusual threesome. He thought he might be getting dizzier because the floor appeared to sway under his feet. Then he passed a porthole and realized he was on a boat- a big one.

"We'll take you to the galley and see what suits you. I hope you like crab, we got plenty of that. I'm fairly tired of them myself. *This guy is too friendly to be a kidnapper,* Li thought.

They walked along together past numerous cabins. The boat appeared to be an old, small, passenger cruise ship. There was paint peeling off the walls and it looked like it had been in disrepair for years. The heat definitely wasn't working and Li shivered.

The galley was a little warmer. There was a stove with a large stockpot with steam drifting out of it. Li smelled the ocean.

"What did I tell you? It's crab for supper again. Soft-shelled, hard-shelled, Blue, or Rock- it all tastes like rubber to me now. I guess this is how the Israelites felt about all that manna." Dave made a sour face and Li just stared at him.

Ellen Cheng, the nurse, opened the large refrigerator and pulled out some bread and cheese. She took a griddle down from where it was hanging and set it on the stove, opposite the stockpot. As she started slicing the bread and cheese, Li walked over to her.

"Why did you kidnap me?" he asked her bluntly. She stopped cutting for a second and then said, "All in good time, Li. Please trust me for now. We are trying to help you."

"Help me? Whatever! If you think my father is going to pay some outrageous ransom for me, you better think again. He won't! He's too busy being brilliant. He might even thank you for taking me off his hands."

Li thought about Ainsling now. His stomach hurt more.

Ellen continued to prepare toasted cheese sandwiches as tears formed in her eyes. Aaliyah walked over to her.

"He'll understand later. Let the Captain explain it to him." She rubbed Ellen's back soothingly. Turning to Li she said, "Young man, we're on your side. Have some faith. After we get some food in you, we'll take you to the Captain and he can explain it all. Come sit down now."

Li grunted and sat down. He crossed his arms over his chest. His stomach growled. Ellen flipped the sandwiches on the griddle. *I guess I have no choice,* he thought.

In a few minutes, she set down a plate of warm food in front of him and he ate it all. His stomach felt much better. Now he wanted some answers.

"Okay, now, take me to your leader!"

"It's *Captain,* not 'leader.' Technically, his naval title is 'Master,' but he insists on being called Captain," Pastor Dave explained.

"Okay kid, follow me!" Aaliyah announced.

The dark woman got up and pushed in her chair. She gave a hopeful smile to her associates. They smiled back in unison.

Li followed her as they went to the Captain's quarters. The door was a thick oak one with a frosty porthole window situated at eye level. Li could see through it dimly. A shadow appeared behind it soon after Aaliyah knocked.

The door creaked open and a short man with olive skin and a scruffy salt-and-pepper beard greeted them. Li noticed he held a cane. *This guy would be easy to take down,* Li thought, inwardly planning his escape. The ocean was going to be his biggest problem. He wasn't much of a swimmer.

"You must be Li! Welcome aboard *'The Remnant'*. This used to be a tour boat a long time ago. I think you'll be quite comfortable here. It's like a floating hotel!

"Who would've thought my sailing hobby would qualify me to captain a real ship? I'm like a kid in a candy store! Enough about me- we've been expecting you, Li."

He hobbled aside to allow Li to come through the door. *"Come into my parlor, said the spider to the fly."*

Li stared vacantly at this strange man with the scruffy beard, extremely doubtful of his sanity. He stepped cautiously over the threshold.

"Aaliyah, you can go. We're going to need some time here." She bowed her head respectfully and closed the door behind her.

Li felt a little uncomfortable to be alone with this odd man. He took in his surroundings. It was dark, but he could make out a kitchenette, a lounge area, and a door he assumed led to a bedroom.

In the lounge area, Li noticed piles of books, some bookshelves with more books, and a table with a drop cloth draped over what could have possibly been even more books. If this crazy guy was the spider, his web was already full...of books, anyway. *I've been kidnapped aboard a floating library. Just great. I bet Ainsling would love it.*

Li had been too busy looking around to notice the old man staring at him, smiling a crooked grin. When he finally turned to face him, he was concerned. Li feared this was his psychotic-old-man-who's-been-at-sea-too-long look. *I'm in trouble now*, he thought, preparing for fight or flight.

Surprisingly, the old man declared, "I remember when you were a baby, Li. You had some wild hair then! I guess some things don't change."

Li hadn't given much thought to his appearance. Glimpsing his reflection in the shiny kitchen cabinet, he now understood why the Captain would consider his present hairstyle 'wild.' Half of his hair had come loose from the band and he looked pretty crazy. He pulled the band out, let his hair fall freely, and smoothed it down as best he could. The Captain smiled and gestured for Li to sit. He went to the sink and filled up a teakettle with water and set it on a hotplate.

"You knew me *when?* What the he-"

"Look, I know you're confused. Let me start from the beginning. I was a scientist 25 years ago. My emphasis was on cognitive neuroscience. I researched decision theory."

The Captain paused to check if Li understood this term. The look of ambiguity on Li's face inferred that he didn't.

"Never heard of Blaise Pascal? 'The Paradox of Choice'? The 'known unknowns?'"

The Captain assumed Li was either apathetic or defiant. His dark eyes were deliberately examining the room, as if he was going to be tested on it later. The Captain gave up explaining.

Li was indeed trying to memorize the details of his surroundings in order to describe them later to E.C.C.O. agents when he figured out a plan of escape and made it back to the city. He was attempting to read some of the titles on the spines of the many books piled around the room. *Leaves of Grass, The Waste Land and Other Poems, Ariel, Shakespeare's Sonnets… Where the Sidewalk Ends?*

"At least I found a career which encouraged my love of poetry," he shrugged, watching Li peruse his collection.

"Now here's the part *you* might care about- I became a research fellow at The Institute downtown. You've heard of The Institute, haven't you?"

Li nodded his head. He had seen it on his father's morose and lengthy resume once. He never talked about the place though, at least, not to him, anyway.

"Let me tell you, son, it was a bad time to be a research scientist! The economic crisis had grown out of control. No one was concerned about curing Alzheimer's or schizophrenia, much less in my 'trivial' psychological studies. In those days, it seemed like we couldn't go a month without a tornado or hurricane ripping through the land. Then, to make matters worse, there were riots breaking out in all the cities. It was a horrible time."

He had a faraway look in his smoke-gray eyes as if he had traveled back in time and could see something Li had only read about in history classes.

"Money for research was dwindling. But one of my fellow researchers vehemently campaigned for funding. He immersed himself in his work, even though the world was going to hell around him. The belief that scientific discovery could safeguard him from anything else happening in the world was what motivated him, I think. Though, who can really know a man's mind? 'There's no art to find the mind's construction in the face.' That's Shakespeare. Um, the red book there," he pointed with his cane at a pile of unusually worn-out looking tomes. Li reorganized his posture as the old man seemed to be determined to pontificate even more.

"He stayed at the lab all day and night, working on covert projects. The rest of us could talk endlessly about our research, but he never said a word. Then he was found breaking our ethical code by attempting to bring in human test subjects without their informed consent. He was fired immediately." He hobbled around on his cane while he talked and stopped right in front of Li.

49

"I suppose you've figured out I'm talking about Jay Griffin, your father, huh?" Li nodded gruffly. He didn't want to give the weird guy the impression that he was interested, even though he was honestly overwhelmed by the fact this man had known his father.

The kettle whistled and the man shuffled over and picked it up. The Captain put some tea bags into two cups and filled them with hot water. The steam wisped around them. Li was thankful for the respite from the story in order to wrap his brain around it all. As the Captain set down the kettle, Li noticed two small scars in the center of the old man's right palm. The scars reminded him of the two parallel lines which denotes 'two' in Chinese characters. He didn't know much Mandarin, but numbers were pretty easy.

He suddenly realized what those lines meant. He straightened up abruptly and said, "You took out your chip? Do you realize what that means? You may as well be dead!"

Li watched as the man raised one eyebrow and gazed down at his palm, examining it like a palm reader. He noticed the man start to smile slightly, one side of his face crinkling like cracked leather.

"Or invisible," the Captain finally responded. *"O for that night, when I in him, might live invisible and dim!"*

Li stared at him dumbfounded.

"Ever study poetry? That's Henry Vaughan. Good stuff. Look, Li- on this ship, we are all in the same boat, both literally and figuratively. Everyone on this ship has had their chip taken out. We are not part of that world anymore. We're free."

"Uh, okay," said Li, struggling to comprehend. "But that woman, *Ellen,* bought something! How did she do it without her chip?" he spit out accusingly.

The Captain's contented face wasn't affected by Li's obvious frustration. In fact, his expression became suddenly graced with tenderness.

"Whatever Ellen purchased was her last purchase before she removed her chip. She's got a gift for compassion, that woman."

Li remembered the yarn store and the soft, vibrant red yarn Ellen had bought to cheer him up.

"She removed her chip, without any anesthetic, mind you- and threw it into the sea, along with your Com."

Upon hearing that his Com was floating in the ocean, Li felt the familiar heat of anger surge through him. But the Captain preempted his harsh response, "That chip isn't just about money, son. Now they can't locate her, even if they would decide to investigate her disappearance, that is. You have a choice to make- you may stay aboard and let the Guardian help you, or you may return to shore alone. If you remain here, you will have to remove your chip as well. But you will be safe and well-guarded. You have three days to decide."

"The Guardian? What exactly do you and this Guardian think I need to be guarded from?" Li asked, still warm under the collar.

"From 'The Devil.' Isn't that what you call him?"

Li looked at him in surprise. "Ellen looked through your Com. It's amazing how she discovered your unique voice command system. It was just by coincidence, or maybe 'providence' is a better word. Anyway, she began speaking in Mandarin and unwittingly unlocked your Com!" He turned towards Li with a look of astonishment.

Li remained stoic.

"She only speaks her native tongue on rare occasions," he explained.

Li felt violated. They had no right to look through his Com!

"The Guardian advised us to make every effort to keep you safe. We had to check it out. Your father-"

"My father didn't try to call me, did he? Don't worry about him trying to find me- he's probably relieved to be rid of me!" Li rubbed the back of his neck and scowled.

"Ellen *had* to get rid of your Com, son." The Captain sipped his hot drink slowly.

Li was in the middle of cursing him out when the Captain interrupted him calmly, but loudly.

"Where was I? Oh, yeah- 'The Devil!' Calm yourself down, son. I know this is difficult for you, but, you need to understand; we are trying to keep you safe from the devil and his evil schemes. I know it sounds crazy, son. But, the Guardian is in the rescue business. Your situation must have been completely irresistible. I only wish we'd been able to save the girl too."

"The girl? You mean *Ainsling*? Save her from *what*? From my father? But he's going to cure her!" Li's frustration was reaching the boiling point.

"I know that's what you think, son. But the Guardian and I suspect Dr. Griffin has again taken science beyond what man should be meddling with. She is his new test subject.

"Unfortunately, he decided to rush things a bit, which upset our plans to get her out. Her surgery is already completed. 'The Devil' has won this battle. She's his for now."

8 The Remnant

This was crazy!

After a lifetime of loneliness, he had begun to feel…good, like Ainsling had declared him during her last seizure. In fact, he had actually been *happy*. Now, here he was- floating somewhere in the ocean on a rundown cruise ship with some crazy cult. What kind of life could he have here?

He had questions that had no answers. *What had become of Ainsling? What had his father done to her? What should he do now?*

He spent the whole next day in his cabin languishing. The next morning, a light tapping on the door woke him.

"It's Ellen. Ellen Cheng, Ainsling's old nurse…and friend. Please let me in. I've brought some food for you."

He wrestled with his emotions a little, but at the mention of Ainsling, his heart softened and he decided to let her in. Besides, he was starving!

Ellen walked in slowly, carrying a tray in one hand and a guitar case in the other. And it was *his* guitar! He rushed over and stopped abruptly before her, debating which item to take from her first. The tray was trembling on her hand, so he rescued it and set it on the table by his bed. Ellen set the guitar case down and breathed a sigh of relief. She smiled when she saw Li scarfing down the bread on the tray. He drank some of the juice, swallowed hard, and mumbled, "Thanks."

"Li, I want to explain something to you, if you'll let me. We were informed by the Guardian you were in danger, and were told to put you on top priority. Ainsling was on our rescue list as well. It is seriously extraordinary you were actually together all that time!"

Li continued to chew his food and avoid eye contact. Ellen smiled slowly as she said next, "I was the one who taught her to knit. She was very special to me, also."

Ellen clasped her hands together and set them on her lap.

"Let me tell you my story, Li. I once lost a child. A child I had longed for. She died before we could even celebrate her first birthday. After that, my husband and I grew apart and eventually separated. I didn't know how I would go on. In my despair, I decided to end it all. But then I was rescued by the Guardian."

She closed her eyes as the painful memories resurfaced. It was a few moments before she had regained her composure and could continue with her story. Li waited silently.

"One night, I went out onto a long pier and stared into the black water. I was about to jump into the same cold ocean we are sailing through right now, when a hand grabbed me and pulled me back. I ended up on a boat much like this one. The people there told me they had also been rescued in one way or another by the Guardian. They made me an offer- I was invited to join them and help rescue others or I could just go back to my old life. They told me the Guardian believes that the act of being rescued gives people purpose and hope. For me, there was really no choice. I was longing for purpose and desperate for hope! So I joined them and made a vow to do my best to help others as I had been helped."

"But you kept your chip in? I thought you had to get rid of it to join this nuthouse- er, boat."

Li was still holding on to some of his anger. It was difficult, considering her sad story. He couldn't help but think, *It's not my fault-everyone has hard times, right?* He wasn't going to let her off the hook for his abduction so easily.

"I was never asked to remove my chip until we were assigned to help with your rescue. Before that, I was useful on shore just as I was. My chip allowed me to support the Guardian's efforts by purchasing tickets for a tour each year that I never went on, which helped economically to keep *The Remnant* running. There are many underground supporters of the Guardian out there helping us. On board the ship I can make use of my nursing skills. We all have a different contribution. Dave was a Pastor on shore, and is now a counselor. Aaliyah is focused on our security. If you decide to stay, you will find your place. We all have jobs here."

Ellen didn't seem like a nut. It all kind of made sense to him, but it was so different from his former life. He couldn't help but wonder what would happen if he decided to stay.

"Have you ever personally met this Guardian guy?"

"No. I suppose you think that's naïve of me. Giving up my old life for the cause of someone I've never met."

"Uh, a little." It sounded utterly ridiculous to Li.

"It is, I guess. What can I say that would make sense to you? The Guardian saved my life. I guess I feel like it's the least I can do."

Ellen stood up. "You have a choice, Li. Your life has been saved as well. What will you do now? Moping all day isn't doing anyone any good, especially you."

"I still don't understand what I've been saved *from.*"

"That's okay. The answers will come in time. You may find your questions will change, too."

She took his hand and squeezed it gently. He felt his icy heart reluctantly thaw a bit and decided to try to be friends with Ellen. But he was still confused.

"How did you get my guitar?" He was in awe at its presence.

"Oh, well, the Guardian works mysteriously!"

Li rolled his eyes and then shivered. Ellen was wrapped in Ainsling's handmade scarf and felt badly for Li.

"Look, I know it's cold here. If you want, I could teach you how to knit yourself a hat someday."

"I might take you up on that. It's more than cold- it's freezing here! Hey- how many people are on this ship, anyway?"

"On this ship, I believe the current count is four hundred and forty. The Guardian runs a whole fleet of ships. They are all old tour boats like this, not too small to navigate the ocean, but not as big as the Carnival Cruise line. Those ships are massive!"

"There are *more* ships like this one?" Li was astounded.

"Yes. Probably about ten here in Sector One. There are two hospice ships, the *Saint Teresa* and the *Joshua Tree*, which I almost went to because they always need medical staff, but *The Remnant* was short on medical personnel, so I came here instead. To be honest with you, I didn't think I was strong enough to be a hospice nurse. And besides, I wanted to be here with you."

Ellen smiled demurely. Li was slightly embarrassed, but inwardly grateful.

"Anyway, they don't usually bring people aboard the way we brought you here, Li. They began by providing 'tours', though they were by invitation only, and, with a few exceptions, once people came aboard, they stayed.

"It's your decision whether or not you remain, Li. If you leave, though, you will be on your own. If you stay, you have the Guardian's help and our support. We are in the rescue business, so to speak. And there is a certain someone both you and I would like to rescue, am I right?"

Ellen winked and wrapped her scarf, the one Ainsling had made, once more around her neck. Li mulled over this information as his eyes remained fixed on Ellen's, well, *Ainsling's* scarf.

"What's happened to Ainsling? Do you know anything?" Li asked her, his concern for Ainsling heavy on his heart.

"Yes, Li. But listen to everything before you react, okay? The Captain didn't feel he should tell you this last night." She paused before continuing.

"There was an explosion at the clinic. A few hours before the explosion, one lone ambulance left the facility. Your father was seen driving it. There would be no need for him to take the ambulance if there wasn't a living patient to transport, right? We are confident Ainsling was in the ambulance with him.

"The Guardian has told us we must wait, so we will. There is nothing else we can do right now."

Li was shocked by this news. Ellen gave his shoulder a compassionate squeeze. She left the room, giving him some privacy so he could work things out for himself.

Li felt totally helpless. What had his father done to Ainsling which would make him run away with her like a criminal? His head hurt after contemplating it.

His dark eyes wandered around the room and landed on the guitar case sitting miraculously on the floor before him. He clicked open the four clasps and pulled up on the lid. The black, imitation velvet lining was familiar, worn in all the same places. The rosewood was golden and the strings were slightly aged. He hadn't played much since he had been Ainsling's caretaker.

When he lifted the guitar, it felt comfortable in his hands. He sat down cross-legged on the rug and started to strum it. It was badly out of tune. Li placed his finger on the proper frets to match the strings to the correct pitch intervals.

As he tuned the guitar, turning pegs and plucking strings, he noticed a weird rustling sound inside the body of the instrument. He bent over the sound hole and examined it inside. There was a wad of paper resting in it. He shook the guitar gently upside-down until it came falling out through the strings and onto the floor. It had been rolled up into a tight scroll with a thin red strand of yarn tied in a bow around it. As he unrolled it, he saw it was addressed to him.

Dear Liang,

Good news! I am going to have my surgery today! The doctor told me he sent you on an urgent errand. I can't believe you are gone on the most important day of my life!

I guess its time to tell you about the red string of destiny. An ancient legend claims an invisible red string is tied between those who are destined to meet, regardless of time, place or circumstances. The thread may stretch or tangle, but never break.

Li, I believe we are tied together. Do you feel it, too? Two people so different, yet, we became friends! It had to be fate- what else could it be?

If you are reading this, I must not have survived. Don't be angry. Just remember I believe in you. You ARE amazing and good!

Till we meet again,
Ainsling

Li could hear her sincere, animated voice drifting into his ears straight from her handwritten words. He supposed that she had penned this is in the event that she died during the surgery. She must have placed it in his guitar, in case the worst happened. He tenderly grasped the red string, wrapped it loosely around his ankle, and knotted it tight.

He had to have faith she was still alive. And if she was alive, he was certain they *would* meet again. The Guardian was his only hope of ever finding Ainsling.

Li decided to stay. He chose to believe.

9 The Device

Ainsling woke up with the alarm. She hit it hard and rolled over, pulling the covers over her head. Her training had been long yesterday and she had muscles aching that she never even knew she had. But she knew she would be punished for being tardy. *I better get up now.*

She grudgingly sat up and slid out of the king-sized bed. She passed a gilded mirror and saw that her short, spiky blonde hair was all flattened in the back.

After a long, hot shower, she was sufficiently awake. The tight, black pants and matching ebony tank top she wore showed off both her muscular body and her ghostly pale skin. She seemed to get paler every day, despite the continuous days of sunshine. She thought about asking Dr. Griffin about it, but decided against it.

It had been one year since the surgery. The doctor was constantly running tests on her, scheduling rigorous training sessions and randomly traveling to new places. This was their sixth destination, a coastal town somewhere in the eastern half of Sector One, she had overheard.

She didn't care. There was nothing to care about anymore. She did whatever she was told to now. Fear, anger, love- they no longer held any motivation.

Her Com beeped and she answered it.

"*Da fu!*"

"Good morning, Ainsling," a man's voice said. "I hope you slept well. You were quite impressive at your training yesterday. I imagine you must be exhausted now."

"Ye-"

"But I know you are tenacious enough to attend all your sessions today anyway, am I right?"

Ainsling sighed quietly to herself, but didn't expose her frustration to the caller.

"I'll be right there."

"Good girl. We'll be expecting you."

Jay Griffin thanked the pretty waitress with a flirtatious smile as she set his coffee down in front of him. Today was full of promise. He knew Ainsling would soon be ready. She had shown tremendous improvement in the last month and her skills were extraordinary.

The device was functioning even better than he had imagined. She had even discovered innovative ways of operating it all on her own. Of course, he could always rely on his special motivational techniques if she showed any signs of rebelliousness.

All in all, she had been easy to manipulate. Her love for her father and her adolescent crush on Li had proven very useful to him. Besides, the device had its own built-in punishment. He would never have to worry about her escaping. She was under his complete control.

Now it was time to put her to work. It would be a difficult decision to make. Her first assignment should be something easy, yet impressive. One of his benefactors might be able to suggest something. He would look into the possibilities. It could wait until after breakfast, at least. He sipped his hot coffee and enjoyed the view.

Ainsling arrived promptly at the facility Dr. Griffin had rented out for her training. She stretched her arms and tried to work out the knots in her neck muscles with her own hand. She'd never worked so hard in all her life.

Before the surgery, she was a weakling. Now she knew a dozen different ways to kill or incapacitate a person and was well-trained to accomplish them all.

Besides, she had the device. She was the future- but she wasn't *Ainsling* anymore.

She opened the door and met her trainer, a martial arts expert known to her simply as Rob. They went through a few drills and the typical exercises. Then they prepared for a sparring match.

Ainsling was half Rob's size. But he was no match for her. After the traditional bow, Rob raised his head and was surprised to find no one there. Suddenly, someone grabbed him from behind and had him in a tight chokehold. He soon lost consciousness and crumpled to the floor.

"That was cheating," Dr. Griffin reprimanded. His voice echoed across the room from the intercom.

Ainsling appeared beside him and shrugged. "Isn't that the idea?"

He chuckled. "Yes, it is. But how do I keep him from talking now? He's going to tell someone about this."

"What will he say? He was sparring with a little girl and blacked out? C'mon, he's not going to be a threat to you. Leave him alone."

"I'll decide who is a threat and who isn't, Ainsling."

She hung her head and said compliantly, "Yes, doctor."

Later in the day, Ainsling joined the doctor in the makeshift lab. It was a temporary lab, but it was fully equipped with the latest security.

Dr. Griffin was excited about Ainsling's newest development. The progress he had made with this subject was extraordinary.

Most of the others had died in surgery. Ainsling had not only survived, she had thrived. Each experiment he conducted endorsed his confidence in the device. Today's experiment would be a big step forward.

He placed various objects made out of different materials in boxes on the floor. He commanded Ainsling to trigger the device. Ainsling focused on a sharp, painful memory. It was the memory of her father's death. She pictured the obituaries notice Dr. Griffin had given her. She disappeared instantaneously.

"Okay. Now pick up each object and try to extend the stealth-enabling device to encapsulate it."

The first object was a blanket. It rose in the air as if on puppet strings. Slowly, it warped like the air above a bonfire, and then disappeared. The result was the same for the other items- the computer, the plant, the diamond necklace, and the mirror.

Dr. Griffin congratulated her and bent down to pick up something. He held a small puppy. It was black and white spotted, fuzzy and nervous, shivering a bit. Ainsling took the little animal in her hands. It started to whimper and her invisible hand calmly stroked its back. Soon it nuzzled next to Ainsling's chest. It faded from view momentarily, but then, the dog and Ainsling both materialized fully. She set the puppy in the box with the blanket.

Dr. Griffin pushed two buttons simultaneously on a silver band around his wrist. Ainsling felt a jolt of electricity pulse through her body. The pain was excruciating. In the past, her seizures hadn't caused her pain, but whatever Dr. Griffin had built in to her device certainly did.

"What was that? Do you *like* this little puppy, Ainsling? Perhaps you lack the proper attitude. If you do not try harder, this cute little dog will be tossed from a cliff into the ocean- by you! Now, focus!"

Ainsling emptied herself of all good feelings, ruminating on her father's tragic life- how he had died in a horrible fire at the factory. Then, thinking about what a burden she must have been to him, she felt herself go numb and was soon too depressed to care about anything. She picked up the puppy impassively and they instantly vanished from sight.

Dr. Griffin smiled. Now for the true test. He spoke to Reynolds on his Com. "You may come in now."

Ainsling set the puppy down again and as soon as it left her, it materialized. She sat on the floor with her knees pulled up to her chest, unseen to the doctor. Her depression consumed her. She had never felt so alone. No mother. No father. No friends.

No Li. He left on the most important day of her life. Dr. Griffin explained to her he had received a call from him saying he quit. Said he didn't want to take care of such a weird little girl anymore- he wanted to be free. She thought they had become friends, but he had abandoned her too. There was nothing left to care about.

Mr. Reynolds suppressed a yawn as he made his way down to the lab. He had recently flown in to this secluded place. He didn't wear his suit jacket, but the gray pants and white shirt were the same as always. He hadn't seen or heard from the doctor for a whole year.

Surprisingly, Dr. Griffin had called him yesterday and provided him with pre-purchased airline tickets. All he told him was it would be worth his time. Then he hung up.

After a year without any word, Reynolds had assumed he had been fired. Surely Dr. Griffin blamed him for losing another guinea pig! The doctor had sent him on many errands that day, one of them being to clear out Ainsling's things and deliver them to her father. By the time he had returned, the clinic was in flames. The doctor apparently didn't want anyone to know where he was.

Now Reynolds would be seeing him face-to-face. Expecting a reprimand, he took a deep breath and put on his poker face. Luckily, it was the only one he had.

The door opened cautiously and a man vaguely familiar to Ainsling strode in. *What was his name?* She had forgotten. Then Dr. Griffin spoke.

"Welcome, Mr. Reynolds. I wanted to show you something. Ainsling, once again, please. Show Mr. Reynolds what you can do."

Ainsling rose lazily and walked over to Mr. Reynolds- *that was his name...* He was slowly turning his neck around, from left and right, looking for her, she guessed. If this man hadn't come to her door to begin with, where would she be now? *This was his fault!*

There was no hesitation. She embraced him. Before he could even think about what was happening, he was cloaked.

Mr. Reynolds screamed.

10 The Mission

"No, Li, this row should be all knitting, not purling. When you work in the round, the right side is always facing you. Some people dislike purling, so they knit everything in the round."

"So, I have to undo all this?" Li looked up at Ellen in frustration. She responded by trying to make a joke.

"Do you know what knitters call it when they undo lots of stitches? 'Frogging'- because they 'rip-it, rip-it.'" Li rolled his eyes as Ellen did a lame imitation of a frog's 'rib-bit.'

"I know, it's silly. Look, we all make mistakes! Don't get too upset about it. Knitters are always learning." Li smirked as she continued, "Knitting, like many skills, has a way of keeping you humble."

Ellen smiled at him as he grudgingly undid the row of stitches he had previously knit incorrectly. She couldn't help smiling. This once angry young man was finally softening. He spent a lot of time alone, or with either her or the Captain.

The Captain had lent him a lot of books, having his own personal library full of forgotten tales. One of the books Li had read was an autobiography of the great neurosurgeon, Ben

Carson. The Captain loaned it to him in the hope he would also, like Carson, choose peace to replace the anger he had carried with him aboard the ship, like excess baggage.

Ellen was grateful it seemed to have helped. Li's character had strengthened and his anger issue was now more like a frustration issue. Ellen became very familiar with his frustration. She was the one Li came to after he had spoken with the Captain and was told, yet again, there was no news about Ainsling.

Plus, knitting distracted him. It also strengthened his connection to Ainsling. Ellen noticed he often toyed with a red string tied securely around his ankle. Ainsling had been a big influence on Li. She had been quite the dreamer. Li was determined to hang on to his dreams now as well.

The only other joy he seemed to find was in playing his guitar. She could hear him finger-picking melodies late into the night sometimes.

Ellen wondered about his mother. It was a shame that she couldn't see him now. He had grown into a handsome, talented, passionate and intelligent young man. She was proud of him, as if he were hers. The Guardian had been right. She had found purpose and hope here on *The Remnant*. Her heart was so grateful for what she considered her second life.

The Captain made his way over to them and asked if he could speak with her, alone. Li was busy frowning as he "frogged" his project, so Ellen got up and walked with the Captain along the bulwark of the deck, the sun still low in the early spring sky.

"He is frustrated."

"Of course he is. He's a teenager. And he's heartbroken. He needs to find a purpose here." Ellen sighed as she looked across the foamy silver-blue waves.

"I have found one for him."

"Really? What is it?"

"I want to send him out on a mission. Do you think he'll accept?" The Captain came to a stop and leaned on the bulwark.

"I think so. What kind of mission is it? Is it dangerous?" Ellen asked with the tone of a concerned parent.

"Of course! *'As soon as there is life, there is danger,'* as Ralph Waldo Emerson once said."

He sighed and continued, "Ellen, you know that every mission is dangerous. Any time we set foot back on shore, we are risking everything."

Ellen's forehead began to crease with worry, and he felt compelled to reassure her.

"Li needs this. I once heard it said that *'Talents are best nurtured in solitude. Character is best formed in the stormy billows of the world.'* He is a smart young man and this job may be just the thing he needs to form his character. Besides, he might learn that others besides Ainsling need his help. Tell him to come by my cabin after supper."

He put a hand on Ellen's shoulder and gave her a knowing look and quoted from a book he wished would always come to his mind,

"Do not worry about tomorrow, for tomorrow will worry about itself."

***

After knocking, the door opened and Li found the Captain standing by his tiny table, drinking tea.

"You asked for me?" Li said apprehensively.

"Yes, son, have a seat. Tea?"

"No, thanks. What's going on?" He tapped his foot anxiously.

The Captain handed Li a picture. It was of a group of scientists. He recognized his father, though he was a lot younger. Beside him was a man who slightly resembled the one standing- well, *leaning*- before him. The man was young, clean shaven and stood confidently without a cane.

"This is your research group?"

"Yep." The Captain sipped his drink. He cleared his throat and leaned over the picture.

"See this guy here? The one with the red hair and Irish green eyes? Name's Mark Yancey. He specialized on the occipital lobe of the brain. I won't bore you with the details, but, basically, the man knew everything there is to know about vision. Anyway, he had a big family- five girls. His wife died recently after a long battle with cancer. He took it hard and starting drinking. Not surprisingly, he lost his job due to his alcohol addiction.

"We've had people checking up on him. If he keeps on the path he's on, chances are E.C.C.O. will soon label him 'unproductive' to the lowest degree. They would confiscate his house and send his kids to a factory. Rehabilitation isn't an option to them, you know. They will only give him his final treatment and leave his children fatherless and orphaned. The Guardian decided to make him the offer. So we're sending a team. Interested?"

"I'll go."

Li stared unwaveringly at Yancey's face. He had to do *something*. He was about to go crazy from the waiting. This mission, at the least, offered him a bit of excitement. He recalled Ainsling confessing to him about her father being a factory worker and imagined how difficult her life must have been there. All due to her sickness. He couldn't let other kids suffer like that.

"What do I do?"

"Whatever the team leader says, okay? If you do this, you have to know the risk. We can't be discovered! There are already rumors of us. People telling stories around the campfire kind of things. But we can't be caught. No attracting attention! Do you understand, son?"

"I understand. I've had training in martial arts, you know. If you need a ninja, I'm your man!" Li grinned.

"This is not a joke, Li. I know you are getting jumpy waiting around here, so I'm trying to give you something meaningful to do. But you have to take it seriously, okay?"

"Fine. I'm serious. Maybe next time we'll rescue Ainsling, right? I *want* to do this, Captain. I need the practice."

The Captain looked in Li's eyes. He squeezed his shoulder encouragingly. "All right, son, I'm proud of you."

***

Aaliyah was the team leader. The rest of the team was composed of three men in their mid-twenties. Li was the youngest of the team members. He was getting excited. After a long, uneventful year, he was finally *doing* something.

Aaliyah was good at her job. Li could tell she was a born leader. He wouldn't dare cross her, that's for sure. He'd been her sparring partner over the past year and knew firsthand how accomplished she was in hand-to-hand combat. He figured that between the two of them, they could surely handle any dangers they faced.

The team divided into two lifeboats and rowed to the shore, stowing the craft behind a wooded area. The plan was that two of them would shadow the other three and be on lookout for any police, security personnel, or E.C.C.O. agents. Li would be one of the shadow guards. Aaliyah located their position and found a route to take.

The Yancey's home was directly along the coast. It was a beautiful, white Cape Cod-style house. It stood boldly on a precipice overlooking the beach, isolated and quiet. Li enjoyed a duet between the wind and waves playing a repetitive, soothing soundtrack. The leaves rustled gently in the tall trees. It was a calm evening.

Aaliyah took the direct approach and knocked on the front door. A teenage girl opened it and quickly let them all in. Li and the other guard stayed behind, hidden by the trees. In around thirty minutes, Aaliyah came out and gave a fanciful whistle. It was their cue to come out and help. The family had packed a few small bags, mostly clothes and personal items.

Li helped the girl who had opened the door with her load. She smiled a curt thank you, grasped her littlest sister's hand and kept her close. The group walked along in silence.

Suddenly, a siren rang out, piercing the calm night. They started to run as fast as they could. The youngest girl tripped and landed face-first on the sandy beach. Li went back to her, bent over and scooped her up. He held her in one arm, grabbed the arm of the oldest girl, who had turned to wait for them, and ran with them both towards the raft.

Two of the Yancey children were with Li and his fellow guardsmen. He assumed the rest of the family was in the raft with Aaliyah. The siren had rushed the rescue of the family and there was no way to know if they'd all made it to the boats. On his boat, the oldest girl put her arm around the younger one.

They were pretty girls. They reminded him of some of the girls he'd known at school, privileged and pampered-looking. The eldest had thick auburn hair under her white cabled hat. The little one was her in miniature.

Li's attention was drawn to their eyes. They had sad eyes. It made them appear older, tired.

His group was the first to disembark from the small boats and gather on the gangplank. He watched as the other boat was unloaded. Aaliyah was not among them.

"Hey!" he yelled to Aiden, one of the team members. "Where's Aaliyah?"

Aiden hung his head and told him Aaliyah thought she had seen someone coming after them, so she pushed their boat into the water and commanded them to go on without her. The last he saw of her was her back disappearing into the dark night.

"Are you serious? Didn't the Captain say we couldn't attract attention? What was Aaliyah thinking?"

He was overcome with frustration. This wasn't supposed to happen! They had left her all alone.

The Captain was soon informed of Aaliyah's sacrifice. He

closed his eyes and subconsciously made the sign of the cross. Li couldn't believe he was so calm about it.

"Shouldn't we go after her, Captain?" he demanded.

"I trust Aaliyah. She knew that before she made her decision. It is possible she will find her way to a safe house, Li. She's quite tough, you know. Even if she was arrested, she would never give us up. I hope that's not what happened; but, if so, I trust her to keep *The Remnant* a secret."

"How can you be so sure? E.C.C.O. is very persuasive. I've heard my father discuss how they can and will do whatever it takes to get results now. He worked very hard to get in their good graces. Don't you understand? Aaliyah might be tortured, in order to keep the precious Guardian a secret. Is it really worth it?"

"Aaliyah knows that better than anyone else on this ship, Li. You don't know what she was before joining *The Remnant*, do you?" he asked.

He didn't. Li had erroneously assumed she had volunteered to join *The Remnant*. She could never imagine Aaliyah in the position of needing to be rescued. She was the strongest person he'd ever met, inside and out.

"What do you mean?"

"Aaliyah was once an E.C.C.O. agent. She became one after living through a nightmarish childhood and witnessing the death of her brother during one of the riots. She once wholeheartedly believed in E.C.C.O. – that they would bring peace. Her mother had raised her and her brother all alone. After her brother died, all they had was each other. But soon after Aaliyah became an agent, her mother began showing signs of dementia. She was being treated by an E.C.C.O. healthcare facility. One day they told her she would have to bring her mother in for her final treatment. Aaliyah loved her mother very much, Li. She couldn't bring herself to take her in to be euthanized. Yes, that's what they meant by 'final treatment,' Li."

The Captain cleared his throat.

"Remember how I said those chips were dangerous? They used the chip to release a poison into her mother's bloodstream. Aaliyah watched helplessly as her mother died. That was when she knew she must go on the run. She miraculously found sanctuary at an old church and met supporters of the Guardian.

"That was a few years ago now. When the Guardian sent a message to Aaliyah and made her the offer, she willingly accepted. She came aboard *The Remnant* and we all became her family. The Aaliyah you know now is a transformed person and she is infinitely grateful. She would never betray us."

Li couldn't respond. He only hoped Aaliyah had found sanctuary and was not in the hands of the enemy.

11 The Mistake

Mr. Reynolds had another nightmare. He woke up in a sweat, breathing hard. This was the third night in a row. The clock glared out the time in bright red- it was 3:33 a.m. He hadn't had a decent night's sleep since the day he'd walked through that door for Dr. Griffin. In fact, ever since the incident that day, he walked in a cloud of depression. His life's regrets nagged at him constantly.

The nightmares were the worst part. Her shocked face, her limp body, and his heavy guilt. The disappearance of her small frame as the doors closed. The baby's cry echoing from the house.

His despair overtook him all over again. It had happened seventeen years ago, but it was being replayed over and over in his dreams these past three nights in vivid detail.

Dr. Griffin had insisted he get a PET scan today. He was reluctant, after seeing (or *not* seeing) what Griffin had done to the girl. Though he had to admit, he was getting desperate.

When Ainsling had grasped him, he instantly felt a wave of cold despair envelop him. Extending her special ability beyond her own body was an incredible feat. He couldn't believe Dr.

Griffin had managed that. It had been many years in the making, he knew firsthand.

But after being an unwilling participant now in his experiments, he no longer rested on the assumption he was protected from Griffin's megalomania solely on the basis of his years of service. He had been used and abused by Griffin constantly over the years, but never so profoundly. Except for one night. The night which haunted him in his sleep over and over.

These nightmares were wearing him down. He was afraid to close his eyes at night anymore, yet he was so tired. He didn't know how much more he could take.

Reynolds swallowed some sleeping pills and slept dreamlessly until dawn. He put on his usual clothes, though he hadn't had anything pressed, so his pants and shirt were uncharacteristically crumpled. He didn't care.

Today was the PET scan. An I.V. was inserted into his arm and introduced the radioactive material, called a tracer. They waited an hour before the tracer was absorbed into his body. The tunnel-shaped scanner relayed the images of his brain into 3-D computer images. Dr. Griffin spoke to him over the intercom.

"I don't need to tell you to relax, do I, Reynolds? I have to say, I am a little amused your rugged passivity has been affected so deeply. You should consider yourself lucky to be involved in my research so intimately. Think of it this way- you are playing a role, albeit a small one, in making scientific history!"

Reynolds had done this test before- when he was hired by Griffin. He did not feel lucky either time.

The scan was over in about thirty minutes. Reynolds returned to his room. Dr. Griffin informed him they would need a few hours to review the scans. He planned to meet him for lunch and discuss their findings.

In the meantime, Reynolds went through the pictures he had recorded on his Com throughout the years. He was seeking one in particular- the one taken all those years ago when he had first started working for Griffin.

Ah, here it was! He opened the file and gazed happily at the picture in his hands. She was an exotic flower, indescribably beautiful, yet trampled like an ordinary weed by the man who should have appreciated her most. He was further drawn to her by the sad fact her marriage had been brokered between her father and Griffin like some kind of business transaction.

Reynolds had admired her from afar. She never treated him like other people had treated him- like a lowly servant. She was kind-hearted and generous. The winning virtues of compassion and intellect led her to become a highly respected veterinarian. He wondered if her job skills also contributed to her ability to live with such an animal as Jay Griffin.

This picture had been taken the day he had made his first mistake while in Griffin's employ. That morning, he had been victorious; he had been able to manage taking a picture of Olivia with his Com clandestinely. She was her usual bright and beautiful self.

That afternoon, Dr. Griffin had asked him to chauffeur Olivia home. She had been visiting at the research facility and whatever happened there had caused her usually blithe face to morph into a tormented one.

As usual, he didn't initiate conversation. After nearly twenty minutes in silence, she asked, "What do you do for my husband, Stanley?"

He paused to consider his reply. Dr. Griffin was working on a covert project and all Reynolds knew about it was that he wanted test subjects- epilepsy patients who would be willing to participate in medical studies for his research. Reynolds was assigned to bring in new subjects without a contract of consent- and then to keep them silent.

Other than that, he merely followed Dr. Griffins' instructions, one of them being he was not to catalog these subjects in the record at the Institute. Dr. Capitani was to be kept unaware of the details of this research project and Griffin paid Mr. Reynolds well to keep it that way. Reynolds assumed sharing this information with Olivia would violate his contract.

"I do whatever he asks of me, ma'am."

"Stanley, do you know anything about his project?"

"I don't have the liberty to share that information," he told her. "You should ask your husband, Mrs. Griffin."

"I have, Stanley. But I'm scared he's hiding something big. He hardly ever comes home now, not even to see Liang." She sighed and rubbed her temples. "I think he's doing something illegal. You don't want to get in trouble because of him, do you? Please tell me and I promise I will help you!"

He suppressed a laugh. *She* wanted to help *him?* He wanted to suggest she needed to reverse that statement. But he remained mute. Over the years, secrecy had become Stanley Reynolds' best skill.

She almost gave up on her questioning, but granted him one last opportunity at coming clean. "Did you know Jay was once a chemist? He seems to be living up to the role of 'mad scientist,' don't you think?"

She frowned, disappointed in Stanley for being so blindly loyal. They arrived at the Griffins' home and Stanley parked the car adeptly and opened the door for her to exit the sleek, black vehicle.

Olivia faced him, her honest face less than ten inches from his.

"I'm going to tell you something I haven't told anyone else, Stanley. I am planning to divorce him."

His ears perked at that. *Divorce him?* Then she would be free? *Maybe...*

"But without something to hold over him, he could easily take everything away from me- my job, my reputation, and my son. My father passed away last month. Jay received his inheritance today, Stanley. Now he has no need to pretend to care for me anymore."

He couldn't believe anyone would have to pretend to care for this lovely, perfect lady. She frowned, and it was almost comical the way her small lips pursed into a pout.

"With all the chaos the country is experiencing, I don't know who to trust. I'm scared, Stanley."

Her hands were shaking and Reynolds understood. She had every reason to believe Dr. Griffin could make her life infinitely more miserable than it was now with just one phone call. He had powerful connections and, if motivated, he would cross any line necessary to protect himself.

Reynolds' own fear of Griffin had cumulatively crippled any moral courage he had ever held. Courage was merely a word now, a vague, lifeless one.

As a last ditch effort to resurrect courage, Stanley Reynolds made his first mistake as Dr. Griffin's subordinate. One he would never forget.

He reached into his briefcase and pulled out a confidential file. It was the application for a test subject that had come in to the lab two months ago. The subject had come out in a body bag and Reynolds had been commanded to dispose of the body by dumping it into the bay.

The pictures and paperwork inside were the only copies left. It was foolish to keep secret files on a computer, where they could so easily be hacked into, so they resorted to this old-fashioned method of paper and pen.

He had been told to destroy it, but hadn't done so yet. He was sure the file would implicate Griffin completely. Alone, it would be enough to charge him with many crimes. He handed it to Olivia.

"Here," was all he said.

She took it from him and held it gingerly, fear and eagerness fighting each other in her mind. The envelope was tightly sealed with thick tape. She turned away from Stanley and used her keys to rip the envelope open. As she did, a powdery cloud rose from it. She began to cough and dropped the envelope to the ground.

Reynolds caught her before she collapsed. He carried her inside the house, where the nanny squealed at the sudden sight of them. She was holding two children, one at her hip, who Reynolds recognized as Liang, and a tiny baby he had never seen before over her shoulder. The baby began crying when the nanny squealed. The pretty blonde nanny patted her back and little Liang reached out his chubby toddler's hand and patted her, too. He spoke to the baby, "Kay Ling, it 'kay Ling!"

Reynolds carried Olivia past the crying baby and ignored the noise. His focus was completely on Olivia, laying her on the couch and propping her head with a pillow. He called 911, but was afraid they wouldn't arrive in time, or even at all, since there were so many emergencies needing attention in those days. He did the only thing left to do- he called Dr. Griffin.

When Dr. Griffin arrived, he rushed over to his wife. He looked at Reynolds murderously, knowing he had betrayed him. He put a mask on her and began to pump oxygen through it. When the ambulance arrived, he got in with Olivia, threw a mask and gloves at Reynolds and ordered him, "Destroy it, you fool!"

Reynolds threw the large envelope into a pot on the stove and lit it on fire. He destroyed the evidence, but couldn't destroy the feelings of regret and fear that would forever haunt him.

Olivia survived, though she was in the hospital for months before her physical wounds were healed. But there was damage to her brain, particularly her parietal lobe. The damage to this area of the brain meant she was slow to recover her speech.

When she finally spoke again, she did not remember Griffin, Reynolds, or even Liang. Reynolds always suspected the brilliant doctor had facilitated this rather convenient memory loss somehow. It was certainly ironic she had been so close to uncovering Griffin's crimes, and now she didn't show any more interest in him than she did towards Dr. Hu, her rehabilitation coach with the obnoxious bow ties.

Stanley Reynolds was profoundly relieved. The fact she could not remember her suspicions of Griffin's malfeasance was what was keeping her alive. He could accept she had forgotten him if it meant she would live.

Dr. Griffin had absolutely no need for her now. He took advantage of the opportunity to remove her from his life, both legally and physically. The hospital helped her relocate to another city. She never realized she was leaving behind her only son, a husband, and a dangerous secret.

Griffin never spoke of her again to Reynolds or to Li. Reynolds, though, would always remember.

It was almost noon. He clicked off his Com and rose to meet the doctor for lunch and to hear his diagnosis.

Dr. Griffin was waiting for him at the bar. He offered Reynolds a drink.

"No, thank you," he replied to the offer.

The Doctor smiled wryly at him and continued to be entertained by Reynolds' extreme depressed demeanor. He ordered some food and then stretched his arms behind his head. His comfort was a stark contrast to Reynolds' discomfort.

"The radiologist and I concluded you are experiencing a temporary synaptic episode. In other words, your melancholy days will soon be over." Griffin smiled alone.

"But, Reynolds, I must apologize. Using you as part of my research without forewarning you was rude of me. It just so happens that you have shown an interesting side effect of my device's cloaking capabilities. You helped me discover that when Ainsling extends the cloaking power of the device to another object, i.e., a person, she conducts electric impulses from the leads in her limbic system, which is the part of the brain which controls emotion. The trigger for the device produces an over-stimulation of the hippocampus."

He paused to check whether Reynolds was following his explanation. Reynolds appeared noncommittal. Since he was simply thinking aloud anyway, he thought he might as well go on.

"The amygdala is the emotional center of the brain. Somehow her extension of the cloak over stimulated *your* amygdala as well. The PET scan shows this. I believe electroconvulsive therapy or deep brain stimulation will be all it takes to get you back to your old cheery self," Griffin chuckled at the thought of a "cheery" Reynolds.

Stanley decided his life had finally sunk as far as it could possibly sink. The waves of dysphoria he had been experiencing, coupled with the nightmares, had left him empty. He nodded numbly at Griffin.

Ainsling marched over to where they were sitting, ignored Reynolds and faced Dr. Griffin.

"What is my first assignment?"

"Well, now, we can't go discussing that in front of Mr. Reynolds, now, can we? Let me explain the details to you in my office in, let's say, an hour. Okay, sweetheart?"

He looked giddy with excitement, or power. Ainsling accepted this response and walked away, never once acknowledging Reynolds' presence.

"Oh Reynolds, cheer up, old boy," Griffin teased.

The server set their food before them and Reynolds pushed it around on his plate. Griffin devoured it heartily and then stood to leave. "I'll schedule an appointment for your treatment after I have sent Ainsling off on her first quest. Try to stay positive until then."

Reynolds took a few bites of his meal and left the empty restaurant alone. He caught sight of Ainsling walking towards him from the hall at the residence Dr. Griffin had rented out. She frowned condescendingly as she approached him.

He recalled the first time they met. He thought about how different that time was from today. The first time they met, she had been living humbly in a tiny apartment with her simple-minded father, optimistically hoping for a cure.

The way Dr. Griffin had twisted both of their pathetic lives was enough to ignite Reynolds to confront her now. He took on an ominous prophetic tone as his empty periwinkle eyes bore into Ainsling.

"Don't let him take all of you! Keep something that's yours alone- hide it in the recesses of your mind or you will lose your soul too! Don't let him take it away! Remember, Ainsling! Tie it to your heart and never let him take it from you- tie it to your very soul!"

Ainsling had successfully dismissed his crazy rant until he said the word "tie." At the word, she felt a sharp pain in the pit of her stomach. She had once believed in the red string that tied her to...

But how could she believe in that anymore? She once believed in so many things and they had all fallen apart. Fairytales, stories, myths, friendship. *Did any of it really matter anymore?*

She continued down the hall and found Dr. Griffin leaning over his computer. He appeared to be preparing her assignment. She cleared her throat and he brought his head up from his work. He handed her the small paperback book-sized computer and went over the details of the mission.

"...you will be communicating with me at the same time each evening at 11:30 p.m., giving me a full run-down of your day, including any details about the person you watch. Our employer only needs intel, so do not take any action or make any judgments. Just the facts, okay? This Com is untraceable, but remember, I can always reach you through the device, so don't even consider 'running for freedom' or any such nonsense. You will never be free again. Understand?"

She nodded passively. The assignment seemed like an easy task, though she'd never had to maintain her invisibility for as long a time as she expected this to require. The time she spent sustaining the device drained her emotionally. She couldn't predict the effect, if any, that it would cause.

Dr. Griffin certainly knew this and was probably scientifically eager to find out. She wondered what kind of threat this person was, and then decided it just didn't matter. Her training would help her with any bodily threat. Besides, it's hard to fight what you can't see.

Ainsling returned to her room and prepared for her journey. She stuffed what little she could into the backpack Dr. Griffin supplied. Going through her supplies, she was annoyed by Reynolds' tirade earlier. What he said had been bothering her.

Everything she was packing now was new, given to her over the past months by the doctor. Everything that was *hers*- all her books, yarn, and blankets- were gone. Her mother, her father, and Li- all gone. She had nothing to tie her to her heart anymore.

Out of the corner of her eye, she noticed a red silk scarf in the back of the drawer. *Should I?* She thought.

Can I really believe anymore?

She decided to take a chance on Reynolds' hysterical advice. He had never shown any emotion whatsoever before this- at least, none she had seen. Dr. Griffin was constantly trying to get a rise out of him, with no success. Even if he was only talking crazy now, she had an uncanny feeling his odd words should be taken seriously.

Ainsling decided to hope again. She ripped a strip of red fabric from the scarf and tied it around her ankle. She tucked it under her sock so only she would know it was there. It was *hers*.

12 The Prayer

"Where's Mark?" the Captain asked Aiden and the rest. The five girls, as young as five and as old as seventeen, hung their heads. The eldest sighed and looked annoyed, possibly even bored.

"He left. Along with our dog, apparently. They've both been gone for a few days. Usually that means he's on another drinking binge."

It appeared Mark Yancey's drinking problem had created a deep set bitterness in his eldest daughter. The Captain noted her sarcasm, accepting it as a typical coping mechanism.

"I see. What's your name, dear?"

"Lisa. Look, thank the Guardian for us for helping us out, but my dad has done this to himself. You shouldn't even bother helping him. He's a lost cause! He's not the only one who misses mom. But he doesn't care about anything else but the bottle now, not even us. If he's gonna be like this, just let him drink himself to death alone- without making us watch!"

With each continually vehement word, her youngest sisters' sobbing grew louder.

"Stop it, Lisa! You're making Sarah cry," her younger sister, Kayleen chided.

"Ellen, take these girls to one of the suites and get them comfortable. I'd like to speak to you Lisa, after you get settled. Will you come by my cabin tomorrow morning?"

Lisa shrugged. "Whatever. Um, good night."

She stopped in front of Li. She examined him, looking him up and down, possibly accessing his outer qualities, and said grudgingly, "Thanks."

He gave her a polite nod of acknowledgment and watched them walk away. Aiden approached the Captain.

"Sir, as we were getting in the lifeboats, there was a siren going off. It sounded like Agent sirens. I'm sure E.C.C.O. was keeping tabs on Dr. Yancey's house. We can't go back there!" Aiden was insistent.

"I know. But, the trouble is, the Guardian gave us a job. We haven't completed the mission. We still need to rescue Dr. Yancey."

He hobbled away and Aiden and Li were left alone in the corridor. Aiden gave Li a tired look, patted him on the shoulder and walked to his cabin. Li then realized how tired he was all of a sudden. The adrenaline rush was over.

Yes, Aaliyah was on shore. But there wasn't anything he could do to help her now. After some tossing and turning, he finally fell asleep.

The next morning, the sun rose early; but Li didn't. He ventured out of his cabin sometime after 10 a.m., headed for the Captain's quarters. He walked quickly along the starboard side deck of *The Remnant*.

Since returning from the mission, he wondered how they would find the girls' father. Self-depreciating drunks aren't very easy to track. He hoped the Captain would allow him to help.

"Hot date?" a wry voice asked him. He turned his head and saw the girl, Lisa Yancey, sitting on a deckchair behind him.

"Uh, no."

"Well handsome, maybe you can tell me what there is to do on this floating dump. I'm bored already."

Li didn't know how to respond. *Didn't she realize someone had been left behind, risking her own life to bring her sorry butt on board?*

Then he remembered he had once felt equally as bitter. But now he felt this ship was somehow...*home.* He didn't think she would understand that yet, and berating her over her ignorance of Aaliyah's sacrifice wouldn't change anything.

"Um, well...sometimes a group here puts on plays and stuff. There was one last week where this short kid, I think his name was Bjorn- something incredibly Swedish, anyway- dressed up as a creature with big green ears who talked all backwards, saying weird philosophical things, and hopped around on a cane. It kinda reminded me of the Captain. Don't tell him I said that, though."

Lisa rolled her eyes and looked at Li as though *he* had big green ears.

"Uh, whatever. Hey, how is this thing even allowed to exist? If E.C.C.O. discovers us out here, we'll all be arrested as instigators or tax-evaders, you know! By the way, if you all don't have chips, how do you buy food and supplies?"

Li assumed she hadn't made her choice yet.

"Well, as far as I understand, there are many people on land who have been helped by the Guardian and have volunteered to help shore-side. You see, this is designated as a tour boat by E.C.C.O. Our supporters buy tickets for a 'tour' they never go on, which they purchase from a company run by the Guardian. This ship is only one of a fleet of vessels. The supplies are purchased legally, though there's not a lot of money left after paying for fuel and all. And we pay taxes, so you can stop worrying about going to jail."

Li had been curious as well and asked the Captain about it his first week on board. Both Ellen and the Captain had openly shared this information with him and it made him feel safer.

The Guardian seemed to exist and work without E.C.C.O.'s interference. It impressed him. He shared with Lisa exactly what they had told him in the hope she would also start to feel secure and safe here.

"I wonder if I could put in a request? I had to leave without a hair dryer," Lisa said dryly.

Li knew she was only making it hard on herself. She was probably used to a much more upscale, cushy lifestyle. He wondered if that was what he had sounded like once. He tried again to reach out to her.

"I didn't want to be here at first either, Lisa. It's hard to adjust. The Guardian seems to have a handle on things, though. Hang in there, okay?"

Li began to walk away from her. He wanted to visit the Captain and ensure he was involved in whatever the new plans were for rescuing Dr. Yancey. Lisa flung around and yelled at his back,

"What makes you think the Guardian is a guy? That is so typical. Male chauvinist!"

Apparently Lisa wasn't about to stop sulking because of one kind gesture. He turned around to face her.

"I don't know. Geez, sensitive much?"

They stood awkwardly on the deck for a few minutes, with the annoying cacophony of gull song filling in the silence.

Lisa began to regret her comments, but couldn't quite manage to think of a cool way to retract them. After an uncomfortable silence lapsed long between them, Li sighed and decided this was a waste of time. He was eager to visit the Captain.

As he took his first steps away from her, Lisa reached out and grabbed his arm. He was surprised and turned back towards her. She had reluctant tears falling down her pouting face.

He said sympathetically,

"It'll get better. We're going to find your dad. I know you're mad at him, but it sounds like he was once a good dad, right?

You're lucky- I never had that."

Lisa sniffed and cleared her throat. She let go of his arm and wiped her face with a tissue, as ladylike as possible.

"Thanks, Li. I guess I'm kind of messed up right now." She looked up at him pleadingly, her brown eyes reddened and tired.

"Please find my dad! He really does need to be rescued!"

He gave her a sincere grin. She calmed slightly at the sight of his reassuring smile. Li excused himself and went to talk with the Captain.

The Captain was not alone. It seemed he had already started to put together a reconnaissance team. Li was let in the door by Aiden. As he walked in, the Captain was in the middle of a speech.

"His oldest daughter gave me a list of his usual hang outs and the few remaining friends of his she knew about. I sent word to the Guardian earlier this morning.

"We must trust the Guardian is already at work on shore and will keep us updated with any news, either about Mark or Aaliyah. I cannot send you all out until we are in synch with the Guardian's plan. *'The waiting is the hardest part,'* my grandma used to say. But wait we must. Please be ready for me to call you when I receive the word. You may go. Thanks, everyone."

Li stood and watched the group of about six men and women filter out. He was then standing alone with the Captain.

"Are you leaving me out now?" he blurted accusingly.

He couldn't help himself. He had just stood in front of a crying girl who had begged him to help find her father and now it appeared he wouldn't be included in the rescue. It made him angry.

"Li, it's not that simple. The mission is more complicated this time. There will be a lot of uncertainties and we will also be working in tandem with those on the Guardian's side who are on shore. I can't put you in that kind of danger."

The Captain's typically blunt manner was tapered by his sincere concern for Li. Li could sense it and it made him all the more frustrated. He knew it would be worthless to argue. The Captain wouldn't change his mind. He had earned Li's respect by always telling him the truth of things without making him feel like crap. He was the opposite to his father in this respect. Neither flattery nor callousness ever left the Captain's lips.

"What can I do? Anything?" He compulsively straightened the haphazardly placed mugs on the open shelves to distract him from his disappointment.

"Do you pray, Li?"

The Captain's tone was more serious than usual. It was a question Li would have expected from Pastor Dave, but not him. He turned towards the Captain and raised one eyebrow.

"Uh, no. Why? Are we desperate?" Li's attempt at a joke made the Captain frown.

"This is one of those times where I want to challenge you to consider seeing life differently, Li."

He paused, his brow furrowed as he contemplated his next words. His eyes searched the room, as if his next words were floating around in the air.

"As a scientist, I was often laughed at. I had come to a different conclusion than most of my peers. A unique worldview. I'll try to explain. You see, the brain is an intricate organ. I spent years intensely studying it, Li, just like your father. It humbled me.

"The brain is full of mysteries that may never be solved. It is a miracle. I developed a great respect for the Creator of such an astounding puzzle. Your father went down another path. He thought, because of all the knowledge he had gained, he had earned the right to manipulate the knowledge for his own benefit.

"We had both eaten from the tree of knowledge. I chose to respect the creator of this knowledge and your father chose to ignore him. You are free to make your own decision, Li, but I sincerely want you to question whether or not your life is in your control.

"I chose to believe that since we are so amazingly made, we must have an amazing Maker. Even after all these years, and after all the scientific research that has been done, no one can explain all the intricacies of the human brain, Li, so He must be above human understanding Himself. That's how I decided to believe in Him. It's a decision which has changed my life, though it has not exactly made it easier."

The Captain chuckled softly at some inside joke. Li was still standing by the half-organized coffee cups, listening to this man he had developed a great respect for over the last year.

He had never spoken to him about this subject before. And Li had already decided if God existed, he would probably be disappointed in him.

"I don't know if you have ever thought about God before, Li. One of my favorite authors, a scholar named C.S. Lewis, once said, *'There are two kinds of people: those who say to God, "Thy will be done," and those to whom God says, "All right, then, have it your way."'* Of course, only you can decide what you believe. But one thing you can do while you're deciding is pray," the Captain said solemnly.

Li didn't know how to respond. He had never been concerned about these things before. Life was life. He knew before E.C.C.O. had taken control, in those terrible days, people had flocked to religion. Soon religion became another E.C.C.O. controlled establishment, and many religious people left Sector One. Many of their buildings were now used by E.C.C.O. for other purposes. Those few churches, synagogues and mosques which remained were under harsh scrutiny.

Pastor Dave had been turned in by his own congregation after disobeying E.C.C.O. by feeding the "unproductives" without E.C.C.O.'s expressed permission. He told Li, though he felt betrayed, he still believed in his God, and human beings make mistakes. He said he had forgiven them, which Li had found difficult to understand.

Out of respect for his mentor and his new friends aboard *The Remnant*, he refrained from responding before he gave careful thought to the Captain's views.

"You could be somewhere else right now, Li, but here you are. Did you ever consider it was predetermined by Providence? Even the Guardian is only a human being. The story goes that the Guardian was once rescued, too. *The Remnant* and its fellow ships in the fleet are the product of the Guardian's own gratefulness. The Guardian is a regular, fallible person who wants to do the right thing. The Guardian believes, like me, there is a higher power we are all held accountable to."

The crew of *The Remnant* viewed the Guardian as sacred. Yet no one knew his name, where he came from, or how he knew what he knew. Li had probably learned more about the Guardian in the last minute than most of the crew knew before devoting their entire lives to this invisible, mysterious master.

"I guess it's possible. I'd never considered believing in anything other than myself before I met Ainsling."

It was true. His friendship with Ainsling had caused him to want to care about someone above himself for the first time.

"She believes in red strings." Li added, causing the Captain to raise an eyebrow.

"Red strings?"

"Yeah, there's a story that says we are all tied to one other person in the world by an invisible red string. And the string may tangle and stretch, but it will never break. What do you make of that?" Li asked with some embarrassment. Red strings sounded pretty silly compared to the creator of the human brain.

"If the string is invisible, how do you know it's red?" the Captain proffered, giving a wink. "It's an interesting view… quite a romantic one. It does acknowledge the idea of our lives being controlled by *something* other than ourselves, doesn't it? Who ties this string, after all?"

The Captain looked at Li, his eyes holding a bit of a twinkle.

"Li, just because you aren't going on this mission, doesn't mean you don't have a job to do. If anything I've said makes sense to you, maybe you should help us out by praying a prayer or two."

Li acknowledged the Captain's suggestion with a "Hmm…" and then rose, deciding it was time to feed something other than his curiosity now.

His stomach growled in agreement. The Captain grinned and commanded him to go get himself some grub. Li left him in his cabin and went foraging for food.

After filling his stomach with the breakfast of champions most commonly eaten aboard the ship-bland oatmeal, Li walked down the corridor towards his cabin. He saw Pastor Dave coming towards him. He made a choice.

"Hey, Pastor Dave!"

"Hey Li! What can I do for you?"

"This is going to sound weird. At least, it does to me, but… Can you show me how to pray?"

Pastor Dave looked a little surprised. He ushered Li into his cabin. Li followed him in and asked, "So, should I get down on my knees or something?"

Pastor Dave chuckled and replied, "If you want to, but it's not necessary."

"What should I say? How do I address…it?"

It was obvious this was the first time Li had ever prayed. Dave found his sense of urgency intriguing.

"Why do you want to pray now, Li?"

"The Captain won't let me go on the mission to find Dr. Yancey. He said he wants me to pray instead. Tell me how, *please*, Pastor Dave!" Both his zeal and his volume had increased with each word he spoke.

"Okay, Li, calm down! Wow, I've never had someone yell at me to teach them how to pray!" He laughed, then smiled humbly at Li.

"Uh, I guess it might be best to start with the standard. Repeat after me." Pastor Dave cleared his throat.

"Our Father, who art in heaven...hallowed be Thy name...thy kingdom come...thy will be done...on earth as it is in heaven... give us this day our daily bread...and forgive us our debts as we forgive our debtors...lead us not into temptation...but deliver us from evil...for Thine is the kingdom, and the power, and the glory forever...Amen."

Li repeated each phrase after the pastor. He took the chance there was really someone to deliver them from evil. Someone who's will it was to help Lisa's dad, Aaliyah, the passengers of *the Remnant*, and...Ainsling.

13 The Withdrawal

"Stop telling me what to do!"

The disheveled man at the bar yelled loudly to no one in particular. The people sitting around him either laughed or ignored him. The noise and the smoky atmosphere provided a hiding place of sorts for the late-night patrons. Another loud drunk wasn't anything unusual.

After the barkeep refused to give him another drink, claiming that he had maxed out his chip, the middle-aged, red-haired man stumbled out into the street, now mumbling to himself. Other pedestrians swerved to avoid him. He made a large effort to walk in a straight line, failing miserably. His mind was groggy. *Where am I going? Home?*

"Mary, I want to go home. I want to go home!"

His wife, Mary, had been dead for four months. He hadn't spent a day since sober. His mind couldn't handle his reality anymore. Continuing to stumble along, he happily imagined his wife walking beside him, as beautiful as the day they met.

"I love you, Mary. You are the prettiest gal in the entire world! What are you doing with me?"

"That's a good question. I guess I'm your guardian angel," a voice replied.

Mark Yancey could see his wife's cute pouty mouth turned up in a wry grin. She was confident and attractive; he was an awkward scientist. He never felt comfortable at a party, but she often held the entire room's attention with her smile alone.

I never deserved her. Wondering about what she would think of him now was more than he could bear. *I need another drink,* he thought.

He walked along the shore, his feet leaving long marks in the sand as he shuffled along. His big, white house entered into his double-vision. He fell to his knees. A strong pair of hands caught him under his arms before he fell completely on his face.

He woke up to the sound of guitar music floating in from a window. There was a strong ray of sunlight forcing him to place his hand in front of his eyes as they fluttered open. His head was throbbing and his tongue felt like a fur ball in his mouth. He turned away from the direction of the sunlight and pulled the covers up to his chin.

These aren't my sheets! Taking a broad look around the room, he came to the realization he wasn't in his own bed. He'd woken up plenty of times on the sandy beach, but he'd never woken up in a stranger's place before. Where could he be?

He was sweating profusely. He tried to sit up, but found himself overwhelmed with dizziness, and layed back down. There was a salty, ocean air smell mixed with the lingering sickly sweet smell of alcohol in his nose. He began to feel nauseous and knew what was coming.

He looked around for something to catch the upcoming vomit. A plastic bucket seemed to appear out of nowhere. At least, he hadn't seen it the first time he'd scanned the room. Thankful and desperate, he dismissed the thought and proceeded to empty his stomach contents into the bucket.

"You're pathetic," an imaginary voice in his mind accused. He agreed. He set the bucket on the floor of wherever he was and fell back asleep. He woke up when he heard a loud knocking.

"Mark, Mark? Hey, I'm coming in!"

A door opened and a shadow fell across the bed. The shadow's owner was a man with a salt and pepper beard, fisherman's cap, and a thick cane. He leaned heavily on the cane as he walked towards him.

"Man, Mark, what have you done to yourself?" The man shook his head, placed his cane on the bed, then sat on a chair so he was facing him.

"We're going to help you, old friend. You really don't have much choice in the matter. Alcohol is a luxury we can't afford out here. You are going to get sober whether you want to or not."

The man's voice was extremely loud and familiar. It finally occurred to him he knew this man.

"John? John Capitani? You must be going crazy. You haven't seen him in almost 20 years! Nah! It couldn't be him..."

He rambled on, talking to himself in the third person. Eventually, he quieted down to a low mutter.

The Captain, or John Capitani, as Mark knew him, placed a water bottle on a side table beside the bed. He sighed at the sight of his former co-worker and friend. The smell in the room became overwhelming. He flipped open another porthole-sized window and latched it.

There was a gentle knock on the door and then Ellen appeared in the room, carrying a bag. She wet a rag and proceeded to wipe the sweat off the man's face and neck. He didn't seem to notice. He was in a delirious state, his body busy excreting the poisons he had been pouring down his throat everyday for months. She took his pulse and blood pressure.

"It looks bad now, but his body will go through worse before it gets better," she informed the Captain. He nodded solemnly.

They left the room together, taking the bucket with them and throwing its contents into the ocean before returning it to the room.

Ellen was on her way out of the cabin again when she thought she heard someone crying. She looked back at the man; he was tossing and turning his head and moaning quietly. *Poor soul*, she thought. His children didn't need to see this. The Captain would hopefully make them wait until he was more coherent. It could be weeks.

They did agree to ask him immediately if they could remove his chip. He may have been monitored because of his family's recent disappearance. After hearing the story of their rescue and Aaliyah's sacrifice, he agreed to the removal wholeheartedly.

Li had heard about Lisa's father being brought aboard and was sworn to secrecy. He tried to avoid Lisa for the time being. The most he saw of her was from across the room in the galley or passing her in the crowded halls. He had been told her father's condition was normal, but normal meant *bad* right now.

Withdrawal was a nightmare to experience, and watching your loved one go through it was like a husband in the delivery room- completely useless. That's what Mrs. Wilson, one of the other passengers, had said anyway. He wouldn't know.

After two weeks of avoiding Lisa, she cornered him on his way down the stairs. She put one hand on her hip and narrowed her eyes.

"Are you deliberately avoiding me or am I just paranoid?"

"Uh, what do you mean?" Li examined the space around her, deliberately avoiding her eyes.

"Is there something going on? Do you have a psycho girlfriend who won't let you talk to other girls or something?" Her eyes narrowed.

"What? No! I've just been busy. The Captain is-"

"Speaking of the Captain, is he around? I want to ask him about this chore list he sent out. I don't think Rebecca should help in the kitchen- she's got a lot of food allergies. If you're not busy, why don't you walk with me to his cabin?"

Lisa didn't bother waiting for him to answer. She took off like a rocket towards the Captain's quarters. He followed her, jogging to catch up.

She was pretty fast for a debutante. She knocked obnoxiously on the door and it opened to reveal the Captain, Ellen and Pastor Dave in the room together. A guy named Smith ushered them in and closed the door behind them.

"Lisa? What can I do for you?" The Captain gave her an obligatory smile.

"Well, first of all, I need to switch Rebecca with Kayleen for kitchen duty, if that's okay. Second, I think the rice we ate yesterday had bugs in it. And third, I want you to tell me why you're all avoiding me!"

She spoke so quickly Li had to wait for his brain to catch up with his ears.

"Lisa, I'm glad you are here. We've been debating whether it was the right time, but it seems you have decided for us. We better tell her, Ellen." Ellen grimaced but nodded in agreement.

"Your father is on board, Lisa. Has been for two weeks now. He hasn't been in any condition for visitors and he's still going through a lot of withdrawal. But if you want to see him, we'll take you to him when you're ready. He is pretty depressed at the moment. Pastor Dave's been great. He's patiently helping him through it. But I believe he needs more incentive. I think if you visit him, he'll be forced to face up to his mistakes and will move past the pity stage," the Captain explained.

"Let's go right now," Lisa stuck out her chin resolutely and began to walk towards the door. Her usually annoying, haughty attitude was her strength now. They all rose quickly and she deigned to allow them to escort her to her father.

Her father answered their knock and smiled as he saw Ellen and the Captain at the door. When they stepped in, he saw his eldest daughter behind them. She locked eyes with him. He felt as if he hadn't seen her in years. He couldn't believe how mature she looked now, and how much she resembled her mother.

Li waited outside. This was none of his business, but he *did* want to see how the guy was doing. He had been praying, after all.

"Lisa, I'm so sorry! I'm so sorry!" He fell to his knees and grasped her legs. He sobbed at her feet and she stood motionless and silent.

"How are you?" she asked finally. She sounded disconnected. Her posture remained statuesque. Lisa wasn't about to lose her cool composure. It was a skill she had spent years perfecting.

"I heard it's been rough," she added dryly.

He stood up, but his shoulders were hunched over as if he was carrying a heavy backpack. He held up his right hand. It quivered waveringly.

"I'm still waiting for the shaking to stop. And I can't get enough water. But I deserve to suffer, Lisa! I have really let you girls down, haven't I?" The pain he felt showed in his face. Li overheard it all and wondered if Lisa would lash out now or keep her emotions in check.

"Yes," she replied. "But you will always be our father. So get better! I'll come to see you tomorrow."

She turned and walked self-assuredly out of the room. Li was still in the hall and she glanced at him briefly as she flew past. He thought their reunion went unexpectedly well, considering the anger she had expressed to him weeks ago.

'Forgive our debtors,' he recalled. That was easier said than done.

14 The Kiss and the Dream

Ellen called out for Li to come in. As he entered the room to see what she needed, there was a loud crash in the corner of the room where a stack of empty boxes had suddenly fallen over.

Everyone's eyes turned towards the sudden sound. Li went over to the mess and tried to set them back up again.

He felt a hand lightly stroke his head and heard Ellen say, "It's okay, Li, it's only a pile of empty boxes. This suite used to be used for storage. You can just leave it."

"Li, we wanted to ask if you'd take the late night shift to watch over Mark from now on. Mr. Yancey needs someone to be here in case he needs anything. Since you have some experience with patients, we thought you would be ideal for the job." The Captain looked from Li to Mr. Yancey.

"Mark, Li's my honorary first mate. You can trust him. He can handle it."

The Captain's endorsement of Li boosted his confidence. He smiled at Mark.

"I'll take good care of you, sir."

Somehow Li was reminded of the night Ainsling had collapsed from her seizure. He felt as if he could actually hear her small voice saying to him again, "Good boy."

He smiled to himself. Her memory always cheered him. Li felt good now. Yes, he was distressed over Ainsling's mysterious disappearance. But in that moment, he had a real sense of her presence.

The red string was firmly tied around his ankle, hidden under his sock, and it gave him peace. There was hope in the thought of their fates being tied together. Someday he would find her. Until that day, all he could do was pray.

After introducing himself to Mr. Yancey, he found himself wandering out to the upper deck to watch the calming waves. He noticed a familiar head of perfectly coifed auburn hair on the lone person standing there. The railing framed the ocean's beauty. But somehow he knew taking in the scenery wasn't the reason she was there.

"You did good, Lisa. I'm sure that was hard for you," he offered. He was trying to be encouraging.

"Did you see his eyes?" she asked. "They were so sunken in. He looks 20 years older than the last time I saw him."

"Be thankful he's quit now. He might get the shakes, night sweats, delusions, and be super thirsty, but he probably didn't damage his liver or his brain beyond repair. I'm going to be on watch with him during the nights for a while. I'll take good care of him, Lisa."

He gave her a reassuring smile. She looked over at him, searched his face, as if in doubt, and found genuine concern there. It touched her hurting heart.

Suddenly compelled, she reached up and kissed him quickly. Just as suddenly, she pulled back.

Li stood there stiffly, like a statue. She ran off before he could say anything. He walked absentmindedly backwards a few steps until he tripped over something, causing him to stagger clumsily.

He shook his head, trying to think about what to do now. He didn't have those types of feelings for Lisa. His heart was already tied to another girl- one he hadn't seen for over a year now.

He began to regret reaching out to Lisa. Obviously she was more of a romantic than she allowed herself to show to everyone. Why else would she kiss him like that?

The door that led into the hallway leading towards the aft cabins slammed shut, causing him to turn towards the loud noise. He blushed with embarrassment, realizing someone must have been there and witnessed the whole scene. *Just great.*

He was starting to wish Carlos was around to give him some advice on girls. He had no frame of reference for this. How could he reject Lisa at this difficult time in her life? He really didn't want any extra drama, either. There was enough already. This ship was like a small town. Everyone knew everything about everyone.

Lisa kept running until she reached an empty suite at the end of the hallway where there was now a makeshift library. She gasped for breath and sat down on a stack of thick reference books.

Had she really done that? She hadn't been able to stop herself! His sweet smile and caring attitude made her lose all reason.

What was strange about the whole thing was that she hadn't pulled back of her own volition. She had been pulled! At least, that's what it felt like...*No way, that's crazy!* After all, her brain hadn't been completely working at full power.

Ugh, what was she going to say to him the next time they met? The thought made her stomach sink. But the memory of the kiss made her float up. It was nice. *He was nice.*

The day continued on until the sun set beautifully over the ocean, as if going underwater for a dip. Li and Lisa hadn't run into each other and they were both relieved about that.

Li went to Dr. Yancey's room with his lightly packed overnight bag. There was another passenger watching him now. At Li's arrival, the man rose, took Li by the elbow and gave him a recap of the patient's condition.

"He's still got the shakes and every once in a while, he claims he sees ghosts. It happens sometimes during recovery-delusions. Just reassure him. He forgets them almost instantly. Well, I hope you have a restful night, but it's a little doubtful." The man attempted to give Li an encouraging grin before he continued, "We can hope for that next week, I'm guessing. There's lots of bottled water in that box over there," he pointed towards the window and Li followed the outstretched fingers with his eyes.

"Make sure he drinks lots of water!" The water was absolutely necessary in order for Dr. Yancey to flush out all the toxins. Seeing this man in such a sorry condition was enough to inspire Li to pray once again, this time for a quick recovery for this ragged looking man.

"Hey, Dr. Yancey!" he said cheerfully as he entered. The curtains were drawn, making the room eerily dark.

"Just call me Mark, okay kid?"

He was sitting in the bed, a worn-looking book in his inconsistently vibrating hands. Li noticed the title, *The Invisible Man,* by H.G. Wells. *What a weird choice,* he thought.

Li sat on the chair opposite his bed. The room was small, but it wasn't the smallest room on board. The boxes from before were now gone, all but the one with the aforementioned bottled water.

The design of the room was simple; all the bedding was white enough to costume a ghost. The walls were also stark white and the floor was covered in golden wood laminate, some of which was worn to the fake grain on the edges.

Dr. Yancey set his book down. His eyes kept playing tricks on him and he decided to give up trying to finish the same sentence for the tenth time. His head was aching. He didn't feel much like conversation at the moment.

"Hope you don't feel like talking. My head hurts." He laid back and covered his head with the white sheet to block out all remaining light.

Li understood. He had brought a project to whittle away the hours if necessary. It was still chilly in the evenings aboard a vessel in the ocean, so he continued pursuing the goal of knitting a warm hat.

Yarn went fast on the ship, but Ellen recently placed an order to have more in the general store on board. Li used *The Remnant* money he'd earned from his jobs aboard the ship to purchase some *yang mao* (wool), as Ellen had taught him in Mandarin, that was soft and springy- perfect for making stuff you wear right against your skin, like a hat. And it was red.

He started the decreases to form the crown of the hat and counted quietly aloud.

"4, 5, 6, 7-"

"Let me be! Stop haunting me! I'm sorry, I'm sorry, please stop following me...I'm sorry, please tell Mary I'm sorry!"

Mark was talking in his sleep, piping down to a desperate whisper.

Li stopped mid-row and looked over at the man. He didn't seem to be experiencing anything more than a vivid dream. *Poor guy,* thought Li. *Losing his wife must've really devastated him.* He couldn't, or rather, he wouldn't think about how he would feel if he lost someone that close.

Once again, he felt compelled to pray, remembering the words of the Captain warning him to take seriously the idea of life being in the control of the One who had created it.

Mark Yancey seemed to be at peace again and was snoring steadily. Li was growing sleepier as the minutes ticked by. If it weren't for the sporadic snoring of his charge, he would've drifted off already. His eyelids fell heavily and he eventually nodded off despite the noise.

Li began to dream. He was walking along the upper deck, looking out over the vast ocean. He saw a person faintly in the distance. As he walked closer, he somehow knew in his heart it was Ainsling. He yelled her name. She didn't respond. He walked faster towards her form.

He stopped when he saw it was not the same Ainsling from the past. She had changed. Her once long, natural locks were now short and spiky and bleached blonde. Her formerly bright eyes were dull and lifeless.

Her face not only held no joy, it appeared to have never known it. She was a shell of her old self. This jaded replica of her caused him to come to a sudden halt.

"Ainsling, is that really you? What happened?"

"You don't care. You never cared."

"Why do you say that?"

"You've forgotten me. I saw that girl."

Li felt a wave of guilt pass over him.

During the whole conversation, she had been looking down, but at this moment she looked up at him. Tears were streaming down her pale face.

Her face was whiter than he had ever seen it. Even her once bold freckles were faint. He was stunned. No words came out of his mouth, and his heart ached like it had never ached before. He felt paralyzed.

Somehow, he managed to form a sentence.

"I miss you."

"Why?" was her short response.

"Why what?"

"Why did you leave me?"

"I made a mistake. My father-"

At the mention of his father, Ainsling's eyes narrowed in anger. He had never even imagined she could look so fierce. He felt a vestige of fear.

"I'm a monster now, thanks to your father! I once believed-"

She stopped and checked herself before continuing,

"I'll never make that mistake again!"

She reached down and untied the ripped red strip of fabric looped around her ankle and dropped it into the ocean. She turned her back to him and stormed away angrily.

"Ainsling, don't leave!" He watched helplessly as her small frame disappeared around the corner. He wanted to run after her, but a voice from behind him yelled,

"Run!"

He turned and saw Mark Yancey strolling towards him, looking past him towards something else in his sight. He came to a stop a few feet beyond Li and began to beg an invisible person in front of him,

"Please, please, run away! If he discovers the truth, he will kill you. He doesn't know that I know. I promise to keep your secret. Just hide. It's all for the best, Olivia!"

He poked at Li's stomach with his finger.

Li woke up with a knitting needle prodding into his stomach uncomfortably. He turned and saw his patient, Dr. Yancey, tossing and turning. *What a crazy dream!*

Mr. Yancey was mumbling incongruently now. He appeared to be finished yelling. Li's mixed up dream left him with an overwhelming feeling of guilt. It was as if he had been sucked into a cave with no hope of return. He couldn't help but wonder why he had imagined Ainsling that way. He worried for her safety even more now. *Where is she?*

His attempts to shake his fears were futile and he found himself defaulting to prayer one more time.

15 The Scar-faced Man

"How are you feeling, Reynolds?" Griffin asked once again, annoyed with this weak shell of a man. He watched him shudder once more. His gray eyes appeared to be looking at some far-away place. Griffin waved his hand directly in front of the man's face, expecting some kind of reaction.

There was none. He gave up.

"It's cold, so cold," he began to mutter, trembling.

It wasn't cold. But ever since the man had been cloaked by Ainsling and rendered invisible for a few minutes, it had damaged his psyche. Dr. Griffin didn't share the fact it was possible the effect was permanent. This realm of neurology was full of conjecture.

It was time to schedule one of the treatments he had suggested before Ainsling's departure. It was at least worth a try.

Before retiring for the evening, he called Ainsling for her day's review. She didn't answer. He decided to be uncharacteristically patient and try again in five minutes.

She didn't answer again.

Now he was angry. He pressed the buttons on his electronic cuff. After a few more minutes, he called again.

"Yes?" Her distressed voice came out of his Com.

"What were you doing? Do not be late again- I will not be so lenient next time!"

"Yes, sir," she responded, the pain from the sadistic electric cuff evident in her voice.

"Tell me about your day," he demanded.

She usually told him everything, with the exception of all her observations of Li. She had kept his existence on board the ship from him the first few weeks, but now decided to divulge part of the truth.

"Li is here."

"What? That's impossible!"

Griffin stared at the Com.

"It's true. He must have been brought aboard recently. I saw him for the first time today," Ainsling blatantly lied.

Honestly, the first time she had seen Li, she was so shocked she had nearly exposed her presence by knocking over a stack of boxes. She reached out and touched his head, his beautiful hair, to confirm she wasn't dreaming.

Now she waited in fear Griffin would notice she was lying. She wasn't used to fabricating things and was doubtful of her acting abilities.

He believed her completely. He was stumped as to how to deal with the information.

"Does he know you are there? You didn't do anything stupid, did you?"

"No! I can handle myself. Oh, there is one more thing. There is a girl here named Lisa Yancey, about 18 years old. The guy I was sent to shadow, Mark Yancey? She's his oldest daughter. Apparently, she still has her chip- I don't know for how much longer, but she has it now. Is that helpful?"

"Good girl. I'll pass that on. You may have nicely saved yourself from further punishment. But listen, you must not let Li know you are there! Remember what he told me when he left? You meant nothing to him. Don't be a fool!"

She frowned and felt all the energy leave her body.

"And Ainsling? Report on time tomorrow! *Wan bi!*"

This unforeseen situation explained why his contacts at E.C.C.O. hadn't been able to locate Li. All those fools sailing on that ship had removed their chips! He must have as well.

Dr. Griffin didn't expect to ever see Li again. It wasn't as if he had ever had the ambition of his foolish son becoming his successor. The boy was, after all, his mother's son, and she had been quite disloyal.

He had considered using Li's feelings for Ainsling to coerce him into keeping his secrets, at the very least, but his good-for-nothing son had screwed up before he ended up having to pull the gun on Ainsling for any kind of motivation. *One less thing to worry about.*

Until now. Li was a lazy and stubborn waste of talent and intelligence. But, of course, naïve Ainsling had fallen for him, and, if he knew anything about psychology, the feelings had been mutual. Maybe he would get to have some fun and use her for a motivational tool after all.

Griffin wondered if his control over Ainsling would be challenged by a fleeting adolescent crush. He'd heard how teenagers basked in the absurd notion of unrequited love, especially silly girls like Ainsling, who had filled her head full of fictional stories and fairy tales.

She must return soon. She could ruin everything! His benefactors would not be happy if his costly experiment did not fulfill its promise.

He had spoken to them inspirationally of a future where they could, thanks to his invention, have the power to watch over their citizens and to instantly act against them. His device offered more power to govern mankind than any other invention before it. He could almost taste his future fame. That is, if Ainsling was truly persuaded Li had rejected her.

"John?"

John Capitani had responded to the title Captain for so long that hearing his first name spoken again sounded strange to him.

"Yes, Mark?"

"I've been having nightmares. About Olivia Griffin."

Hearing *that* name again was even stranger to his ears than hearing his own. He hadn't heard it in years, though he thought about her often, especially recently.

"Olivia Griffin? Why would you have nightmares about her? It's been nearly twenty years, Mark. It was a regrettable tragedy. No one expected that. You are certainly not the one to blame."

He really wanted to change the subject.

"But John, I can't help worrying about her child. You remember, that cute little boy? What do you think became of him? I can't imagine being raised by that egomaniac! Mary used to babysit for Olivia sometimes when she worked late nights at the Veterinary Clinic. Of course, that was before Jay hired a nanny and turned reclusive."

He was opening a bottle of water and took a long drink. "You know it was him, right? He did something to her that night! That robotic assistant- what was his name? Ray? I am certain he knew something!"

He looked intensely into the Captain's eyes and continued, "I've kept a secret for a long time. Now that I've turned my life around, I want to make amends for some of the wrongs I've done to others, even before I was a fall-down drunk."

John could see the sincerity in his old co-worker and friend's face. He frowned.

"I need to find her son, John! He has to be around 18 years old by now. Do you think the Guardian can help?"

John sighed and turned away from Mark, contemplating over what the right thing to do would be. He decided to disclose the truth to his old friend.

"I've already found him, Mark. He's on board the ship. You remember Li, don't you?"

Mark gasped and grabbed the Captain's arm as if he was in danger of fainting.

"Well, that is…wow, I ought to be happy, but now I am a little afraid, honestly."

He began fighting with his thoughts. "He might hate me- but I have to tell him."

"Tell him what?" John was starting to feel apprehensive. What could Mark know about Li that would be as life-changing as what *he* had kept from him?

"What does he know about his mother?"

"He won't talk about her, but I'm pretty sure he doesn't know about the incident. I don't suppose Jay volunteered the fact that he tried to murder Li's mother."

John felt guilty about keeping this tragedy from Li, especially when Li trusted him so much. He had grown to think of Li as his own son now, but he had his reasons.

"That's not the only thing he doesn't know," Mark spilled out, his words flowing uncontrollably like a rushing river, "I might be the only one who does! Before the cancer took her, Mary made me promise to find him and tell him, but I was too depressed to follow through. *I have to tell him, John!* I promised Mary."

His green eyes were wet with tears. John was curious what his secret was, but didn't satisfy his curiosity by prodding. He had secrets of his own he needed to keep.

"Look, I understand that it is important to you, but I am sending Li on a rescue mission tomorrow. Can you wait to tell him until after he returns? I need his head to be clear for this mission." John gave his old friend a few moments to consider.

"Well, I suppose it can wait a little longer," he responded.

The Captain smiled at him and felt a pang of relief. There was only one thing left to do. He went to visit Li.

Li was ecstatic over the prospect of going on another mission! It had been a few days since the unexpected kiss from Lisa and the haunting nightmare about Ainsling. Now that he had something to do, he could procrastinate a little longer about dealing with Lisa.

He also hoped this would help his mind to focus and help to keep his nightmares at bay as well. He packed a few things and went to the gangplank to meet up with the rest of the team.

When he arrived, a fellow passenger named Todd was handing out pictures of the person they were to rescue. Li studied it. It was an older man, with a badly scarred face. He must have been a victim of a fire or been burned by acid. He wore an old, weathered knit cap. They were told they could find him at a homeless shelter, with the address and a map attached.

The problem they faced was that all the homeless shelters were run by E.C.C.O. They had to find him, make him the offer and bring him to the ship without causing suspicion or being noticed.

They were all given scruffier clothes and told to leave anything that identified them behind- pictures, letters, etc...

When they arrived on shore, they decided to split up. Li and Todd stayed together and the two remaining members teamed up. They decided on a rendezvous point and parted ways in search of the scarred man.

Li walked the dirty streets of the city avoiding the eyes of each face they passed until they reached the shelter. They had arrived around suppertime and a line had formed outside. Men and women stood there in clothes resembling overgrown rags. The children were holding on tightly to their parents. Li tried not to let the smell get to him.

"Li, I think that's him!" Todd whispered sideways at Li. Li looked in the direction Todd's eyes were facing and saw a man with a face that was half smooth and half scarred. He was sure it was the man.

"How do we approach him?" Li asked. They couldn't take the chance of being overheard.

"The Captain told me we should tell him we knew his daughter, who passed away about three months ago. He said he would trust us then," Todd explained.

"What if he asks us questions about her? Like, her *name*, for instance?" Li wondered.

"The file said he can barely talk- whatever caused the scars on his face damaged his vocal chords, I guess. Poor guy. Follow my lead." Li nodded and followed him as he sauntered over to the scar-faced man.

"Hey- I think I know you," he began, "at least, I knew your daughter. I'm sorry to hear about her passing. My friend and I here were just going to get some grub down on 83rd Street. It's turkey night there. I'm a little afraid of the meatloaf here. God only knows what they make it out of." He smiled a sincere smile. Li was impressed with his people skills. Todd would have made a fabulous salesman. On *The Remnant*, he was a math teacher.

"Do you want to come along with us?"

At the word daughter, the man's eyes had brightened. His damaged face kept him from being able to display much emotion. But his eyes were still limpid and showed his inner happiness.

In a gruff, scratchy voice he asked, "She make that?"

He pointed up at Li's skullcap he had knitted for himself. Li played along and said, "Yep. She sure did!"

The man tried to smile. The Captain had been right; the man had a very hard time speaking. The two young men felt pity for him.

They started to walk together down the street and came to a deserted park. The swings made an eerie creaking sound as they swayed back and forth on their chains. Todd felt this would be the best chance to talk freely.

"Sir, have you heard of the Guardian?" he asked. The man nodded slowly, his eyes lighting up.

"The Guardian has sent us to help you. We would like to invite you to come aboard our ship with us and be free from E.C.C.O. You will be asked to have your chip taken out. If you do that, you will not be able to change your mind and return to your life here, though. Do you understand?"

Todd waited patiently as the information sunk in. The man nodded confidently.

"Would you like to do that? To be free?"

Todd had a sincere, friendly demeanor and it was hard for Li to imagine anyone saying no to him. The man took a deep breath, and after a jagged cough, replied, "Yes!"

Li couldn't believe how easily that had gone. They had one hour till they had to meet the rest of the group, so they decided to walk along the streets and blend in with the rest of the throng until then.

They rounded a corner and walked right into an E.C.C.O. agent. Todd apologized profusely, but averted his eyes. He was an ace at amiability, but a rookie at deception. The agent looked at them suspiciously, and grimly demanded to scan their chips.

They were about a block from the shelter and the agent must have assumed they were headed there for food. All the shelter's recipients had to have their chips scanned before receiving their small rations. The scarred man stepped forward and held out his hand, palm-up, for the agent to scan. After he did, the man started to cough uncontrollably and staggered around, bumping into the agent and bringing attention to himself.

Todd and Li heard the man mumble the word, "Run!"

They sprinted off. The agent took off after them, but tripped over something at his feet and fell, hitting his head on the sidewalk.

The man sighed as he rubbed the leg he had stuck out to trip the agent. He waved wildly, making ape like noises, and caught Todd and Li's attention. The agent lay there unconscious, so they waited for the man to catch up with them and then ran together to get as far away from the scene as they could. They headed quickly to the rendezvous point.

On the small boat back to *The Remnant*, the man and the crew laughed about what had happened. The man could barely move his scarred mouth into a smile, but Li could see it in his eyes.

"These missions are never boring!" Todd exclaimed.

The man chuckled heartily and leaned over the side to put his hand in the cool ocean water. Suddenly, he lost his balance and toppled in like a ragdoll.

Li immediately dove into the water and felt a burst of wet iciness. The water was cold and black. He surfaced and scanned the horizon for the man. He heard a lot of splashing coming from his left and swam towards the sound.

The man was floundering around, but Li came along behind him and threw one arm under the man's armpits and used his other to pull them both back to the boat. The man relaxed and allowed himself to be dragged. The rest of the crew pulled them up and wrapped their jackets and shirts around them and tried to dry them off.

It was a short trip back to the ship, fortunately, and they were the first to board. Li led the man to a room where they all found some dry towels and wrapped themselves up in them.

"You saved my life," the man said, his voice gravelly, like that of a lifelong smoker, "Thanks."

"Just returning the favor," Li said, still shivering.

"The Lord reached down from above and took me; he pulled me from the deep water," Todd quoted dramatically, smiling wide like a big kid. They laughed together in relief.

The crew accompanied Li and the man to Li's cabin. After they left, Li found the man some warm clothes that seemed to be his size and showed him how to work the shower. Once the man had showered and changed, he fell fast asleep on the other twin sized bed in Li's small cabin.

Li was still shivering. He wiggled out of his wet, fishy-smelling clothes and took a long, warm shower. He crawled into his bed and pulled the covers up to his ears and fell soundly asleep.

16 The Monster

While Li was out on the mission, Lisa had to make a concentrated effort not to obsessively worry about him. She volunteered to take her sisters out to explore the ship. They demanded she take them to the spa first.

The old spa was run by a beautiful Latina woman named Mariposa who had been aboard the ship for two years. Before joining the ship she had been a very gifted stylist whose unbridled love for conversation had caused her to fall into trouble with E.C.C.O.'s laws against dissention.

The girls decided to get their hair cut and styled and have manicures. They were giddy with excitement.

 Lisa took her turn last. Mariposa began to wash her hair and complimented Lisa on her thick, auburn locks. She lathered her hair with some strawberry scented shampoo and grabbed the sprayer to rinse out the foamy bubbles.

The water shot out suddenly and Lisa screamed. It was burning hot!

Mariposa stopped spraying immediately and apologized, both in English and Spanish, swearing she had checked the temperature. She was sure it was set lower. She continued apologizing as she walked towards the back room to check the thermostat. Lisa heard one of her sisters laughing behind her, though she couldn't tell which one it was in order to reprimand her.

"You think that's funny, do you?"

"No, Lisa, I don't! *Lo siento!* I'm sorry!! I promise it'll never happen again!" Mariposa responded as she walked back to Lisa. She continued talking to herself in Spanish while Lisa thought, *Seriously, I wish I were an only child!*

Aloud, Lisa said, "I'm okay. Anyway, I wasn't talking to you, Mariposa."

Mariposa smiled politely, but didn't understand who else Lisa thought she was talking to. Rumor had it Lisa was a little overbearing.

As Lisa was getting her nails done, Mariposa's assistant noticed Lisa had a band-aid on her right palm.

"You've had your chip removed! I'm so glad you have decided to stay here with us here, Lisa. You'll see, it's worth it!" Lisa smiled politely.

The sisters had fun together just being girls. The youngest had previously been quite sad and had stopped talking. But her laughter was the loudest as they got pampered at the salon. Lisa hoped her father would be well enough soon to be a real father to them again, as they had wished for since their mother's death.

She didn't want to get her sisters' hopes up yet. Her father still had some healing to do. Besides, she had been their mom and dad for so long. It was hard for her to imagine him as their dad anymore.

They decided to visit the Chief Engineer and get a tour of the inside workings of the ship. Lisa's thirteen year-old sister, Kimberly, wanted to know if they would have to write a report about it. She was the studious one of the bunch. The ship's school was supervised by a former university professor and she was his top student. The other girls groaned and teased that she was being a teacher's pet. Kimberly, as usual, shrugged off their comments and took notes just in case.

After they explored the engine room, which was deafeningly loud, they were given a lesson on how ships move, as they walked through the bowels of the ship. Bored to tears, Lisa's attention wandered. Then she noticed something odd.

On one of the walls in a dimly lit corner of the room they passed were vertical columns of black lines and boxy pictures. Lisa ducked in the room for a quick look. At closer examination, Lisa guessed it was Asian calligraphy, large, as if written with a crude paintbrush. It was impressive, encompassing the entire wall.

Examining the writing had caused her to be left behind by the others. She ran to catch up with them, but tripped suddenly outside the cacophonous engine room. She went down hard and felt a distinct 'crack' when she landed with her full weight on her left arm. She had reflexively attempted to catch herself.

Amid the clamor from the engine room, Lisa thought she heard laughter. She searched the space around her, but there was no one there.

Then the pain became excruciating and she started to cry. After realizing they couldn't hear her, she screamed with all her might for help and soon the Chief and the rest of the gang came running towards her. She was taken to the infirmary, where Ellen and the doctor on duty used their ancient x-ray machine and determined that it was indeed broken.

"At least it's a clean break," Ellen said, trying to project some optimism onto the frustrated and hurt girl. Lisa let out an annoyed breath and frowned, her pink lips in a pout.

"I am having the worst year *ever*," she declared. Ellen went to prep the cast materials. As she and another nurse helped wrap Lisa's arm, Lisa remembered the writing on the wall down in the engine room.

"I saw something weird on the ship today, Ellen." She winced a little as she sat up.

"Try to stay still, dear," Ellen replied. Lisa grimaced again but continued, "Someone painted on the walls near the engine room. It looked like… like Japanese graffiti or something."

"Really? You'll have to show me sometime."

They finished up with Lisa's arm and gave her all the usual instructions, like "keep it elevated" and "keep it dry." Ellen went out to the reception area to retrieve the medical records for Lisa to sign.

Lisa still couldn't believe her bad luck. Then she wondered if she should ask Li to sign her cast. She felt embarrassed at the idea.

"So, Li, could you sign my cast and, by the way; can I kiss you again?" Lisa said mockingly to herself.

As she was waiting there she felt a yank on her hair in the back. It really hurt! She assumed it was one of her sisters playing a prank and turned around to tell her off, but there was no one there!

Lisa narrowed her eyes and looked around, confused. *Sneaky little brats!* She rubbed the back of her head with her right hand. When she was done she leaned back and closed her eyes.

"I really need a nap," she announced to no one in particular.

Ellen stepped back into the room and had her sign the log. *'Lucky I'm right-handed,'* she thought. She took the pen from Ellen and signed her name on the line.

She was almost out the door when Ellen called to her, "Lisa! Your band-aid came off!" She had picked it up off the floor and was throwing it in the trashcan.

"Oh, uh, thanks. I'll get a new one back at the cabin." She walked a little faster towards the passenger cabin area.

She glanced at her right hand. There was no second scar there. She had wanted everyone to think she had removed the chip so they would stop asking about it. She was too cynical to completely commit. *What if the Guardian, like, died? What would become of them?* She wanted to have some way to return to her old life if this didn't work out. Her open hand closed into a fist and she continued on.

Lisa shared a suite with her four sisters. They had continued on with the tour and were planning on hanging out on the upper deck afterward. Lisa didn't feel much like touring anymore. She decided to rest until they returned. It was almost suppertime anyway. As she entered the room, she noticed right away that something terrible had happened. The whole suite looked as though someone had gathered all their belongings and handed them to a tornado to hold.

She started picking up clothing and straightening lamps and furniture. Some of her clothes were in the bathtub. They had been cut into a million pieces! *This is the shirt I was wearing the day I visited my dad on the ship for the first time,* she remembered. It was also the day she had so boldly kissed Li.

She found a garbage can and filled it with her ruined clothing. Wait until she told the Captain there was someone on his precious ship that was a criminal!

Lisa's bad day had just kept getting worse. She desperately wanted to lie down and take a nap. She cleared off a bed and propped up some pillows to elevate her injured arm. It wasn't long before she was snoring away.

Cloaked and invisible, Ainsling stared down at the petty, ignorant girl. She hated her. Lisa had everything that had been taken from her- a father, a family, a safe place to live, and her best friend. But she remained snobby and ungrateful. Just looking at her perfect hair and flawless face made her blood boil!

Ainsling had obeyed her every instinct today. She had no feelings of remorse or pity. The scalding, the hair pulling, and the tripping were all results of her unbridled emotions. The longer she was cloaked, the less connected she was to her cognitive processes. It was as if she had no rationality. She acted upon her desires alone, like an animal. Reason was no longer a part of the process. She had become a sociopath.

The actions she had taken had been intentionally meant to cause pain, yet Ainsling herself felt numb. As Lisa snored away, oblivious to her, Ainsling was overwhelmed by the desire to eliminate her.

She quickly conceived a plan to hold a pillow over her face. She didn't even consider *not* doing it. She extended her cloak to envelop the pillow as well, and placed it solidly over Lisa's face. Lisa lay still for a few moments, but then stirred and struggled against it.

The sound of giggling and teasing was drawing louder and louder until it was obvious Lisa's sisters had returned.

Ainsling was running out of time to complete her task. She had resorted to sitting over Lisa and holding her down with her legs as she held the pillow tightly against her face. Lisa had started to give up fighting and her skin was now a grayish blue.

The noisy girls bounded into the room, diverting Ainsling's attention. She reluctantly released Lisa from her stranglehold and jumped off her, running out the open door. Lisa coughed uncontrollably. Ainsling ran until she located an empty cabin, then went in and closed the door behind her.

She released the cloak and fell to the floor exhausted. Then an immense wave of guilt crashed into her mind.

She had tried to kill someone! How could she do that?

Ainsling's mind answered back, *'Because you're a monster now!'*

She broke down in fits of sobbing. She could not stop the onslaught of emotion. It was as if a massive wave rose and overtook her, pulling her under the ocean.

Her salty tears were all she could offer to atone for this reprehensible act. When her eyes exhausted themselves of fluid, she began gasping and hiccupping instead.

There was a gentle knock on the door.

"Hello? Is everything all right in there?"

Ainsling recognized the voice. It was her old nurse, Ellen Cheng, her sweet, compassionate mentor. The sound of her voice broke through the stranglehold of suffering in Ainsling's heart. She choked down her sorrow and attempted to breathe steadily. She certainly didn't want Ellen to enter and find her here. *How could she face Ellen like this?*

Ellen didn't open the door, but added, "Whatever it is, I pray you will find peace soon."

After those charitable words, she left, her light footsteps fading away. Ainsling wondered if she could ever know peace. She had already resigned herself to a life of being a slave. *Could slaves possess peace?*

Mentally and physically exhausted, Ainsling fell asleep on the floor of the empty cabin, curled up in the fetal position and covered by a large blanket. Her sleep was trespassed by nightmares and stained with guilt. And the monster chasing her *was* her.

The sounds of loud footsteps outside the door halted her fitful nightmares. She gave up on sleep and opened the door a crack. A group of men were hurrying along. Two of them had their heads draped with clothes, and were dripping water as they swiftly walked down the hall, leaving a salty ocean smell in the air.

She looked around cautiously and decided it was clear. Unwilling to risk letting the monster out, she traipsed down the hall far behind them without cloaking herself.

The men stopped at a cabin and the two sopping wet ones entered. The others said their goodbyes and departed. Ainsling kept her head down as they went by, hoping they wouldn't stop to chat. They were too busy talking with each other to pay attention to her. After they passed by, she examined her surroundings.

This was the middle deck. Port was left and starboard was right, when facing the bow of the ship. Bow and stern meant forwards and aft meant backwards. She had absorbed much of this during her days in hiding, and she knew she was near Li's cabin, which was portside and aft.

She had spent most of her time in the opposite end of the ship, staying in close proximity to Dr. Yancey's accommodations. There she had found an empty cabin nearby to shower in and to avoid detection. She had made her daily reports from that vacant room each evening. The old ship seemed to be at only half-capacity. Ainsling was relieved by that, as it made living incognito more achievable.

A noise from the other direction scared Ainsling and she reflexively cloaked. *Maybe it was only someone slamming a door.* She waited a few minutes to be safe. There was a whooshing sound of the shower running in the cabin she suspected was Li's. She sat on the floor, leaning her small back against the wall and feeling numb once again.

The coast seemed clear now, so she decided to let go of the cloak. Instantly, she felt like herself again. She could feel the sting of pain and guilt, but it was those same feelings which kept her sane now. The overwhelming emotional rollercoaster she had been on after the incident with Lisa had braked to a slower crawl.

There was nothing but silence coming from the cabin now, and she felt drawn to it. She glided over and stood meekly in front of the cabin door. Li's door.

Was Li on the other side of that door? Was he sleeping? Dreaming? She remembered the last time she saw him. She had been so hurtful to him. Maybe he had forgotten it, or dismissed it as just a strange dream.

Ainsling did not consider herself to be in love with Li, but she felt intrinsically connected to him, which was a feeling that was different from romantic love, yet equally strong. Somehow, she felt they needed each other. But that kiss made Ainsling suspect their special connection could be lost. She had reacted more harshly than she should have. She had shown such bitterness and jealousy then, and now, with the help of the device, it had almost turned her into a murderer.

What more was she capable of? She was now deeply fearful of the monster lurking inside of her. What if the device took away everything that made her human? What does a person become when they can't control their anger, their pain, and their actions? An animal?

The door knob turned suddenly, and before Ainsling could cloak, a man exited the room and walked right into her. She tried to act like she had just been casually walking down the hallway, and without looking up, mumbled, "Excuse me."

The man's scratchy voice attempted to reproduce the same words. The odd-sounding voice made Ainsling curious to see who it belonged to, so she looked up.

As she surveyed the man, she took in the scarred side of his face first and then compared it to his unaltered side. The man lifted his eyes, too, and they simultaneously cried out as they recognized each other.

"Ainsling?!?"

"Papa?!?"

Just then, the Captain hobbled around the corner and halted behind Ainsling. She saw her father glance past her and turned around to see who was there.

The Captain bowed his head at her.

"Well, I came to welcome our new rescue. Now I believe we have another?"

Connor Reid was in disbelief at what he thought he had seen, but it appeared this man could see her as well, so maybe he wasn't dreaming.

"Ainsling? Not…dead!" he rasped.

17 The Guardian's Message

"Okay, Reynolds, here's the deal. The goal of electroconvulsive therapy is to induce a therapeutic seizure for at least fifteen seconds. It will reverse the toxic effects of depression in your temporal lobe.

"This was always my favorite field of study when I was a young researcher! I even developed a special technique of my own. You have been a witness to the results of this technique, though you're too simple-minded to comprehend it. Of course, that's one of the reasons you are my favorite employee," he spoke condescendingly to Reynolds as he continued his monologue. He was in good spirits while prepping Reynolds for the procedure.

Reynolds always knew Griffin considered him to be a mindless minion. He had spent years vapidly obeying his demands. He had once believed his loyalty would protect him from being the object of Griffin's cruelty.

But now he knew Griffin was capable of capriciously sacrificing him if necessary in his lust for power. *This ECT may be a creative attempt to get rid of me,* he wondered.

One thing nagged at him- the doctor's mention of his "special technique." *He had been a witness? When?*

Then he realized the truth of the statement. *Olivia*. Griffin had circumvented nature and deliberately damaged Olivia's brain! Reynolds had finally heard his confession. Though it sounded like science fiction, he had admitted he had the ability to erase specific memories.

The effect of ECT on the memory was something Reynolds had researched secretly over the years that had passed since Olivia's disappearance.

Retrograde amnesia was a possible side effect. The people affected by this type of amnesia lost memories of the events prior to treatment, possibly going back to years beforehand. Anterograde memory loss is limited to the occurrence of the treatment itself or shortly afterwards. Some people end up with persistent losses of memory, while some recover parts over time.

Though these were usually *rare* side effects, Reynolds had confidence in Dr. Griffin's medical ability (and in his motivation) to tweak the odds.

It was a verification of his severe depression that Reynolds allowed himself to be treated. He disregarded the possibilities, as treacherous as they could be, because he had lost all concern for his own life now. His willingness to be Dr. Griffin's patient despite the facts could well be labeled under 'suicidal tendencies.'

He went willingly into Dr. Griffin's care like a lamb to the slaughter, his face displaying its usual phlegmatic façade.

Griffin's face held a devilish smile as he connected the electrodes to Reynolds' head.

***

Aaliyah received the bowl of hot soup gratefully. The dilapidated church was dark and damp, with a musty, thick atmosphere. It had been almost three weeks since she had been separated from the group.

She was now in the very same church she had first found refuge in that day years ago, when she had escaped the prison transport. It was hard to believe it was still standing. To her benefit, and probably many others, this church had somehow avoided E.C.C.O.'s scrutiny.

Even for her mother, Aaliyah hadn't been able to fight the system. In her youth, she had joined E.C.C.O., believing they would bring peace.

Unfortunately, the peace they brought left no room for compassion. Their rules were minimal at the beginning, but each year they grew more and more legalistic. Power then corrupted them.

While in prison and alone in the world, hope surfaced when the Guardian sent a message to her and made her the offer. Though she hadn't been able to save her mother, she had been given a new life she now used to save others.

The twin scar lines on her right palm were symbolic of freedom to her. She smiled as she looked down at them. They were a souvenir of her new life. Pastor Dave once said to her, *"The thief comes only to steal and kill and destroy. God made a way so we could have life, and have it abundantly."* That was what the Guardian had helped her find. Abundant life...life with meaning.

During the rescue, Aaliyah had seen movement in the trees while they were all piling into the boats to return to the ship. She made a split second decision to send them off and stay back to either fight or distract whoever it was that had responded to the alarm.

After the boats were in the water, she cautiously edged the perimeter to assess the situation.

All was quiet when she was bulldozed to the ground by a huge mass. It knocked the wind out of her.

She was struggling to pull out her knife that was attached to a belt around her waist when the huge mass panted several rank dog-scented breathes into her face and then proceeded to lick her face affectionately.

"Ew! " she exclaimed as she wiped the dog drool off.

Wondering if this huge, yet friendly canine was accompanied by E.C.C.O. field agents, she patted the big dog's muzzle and found its collar and tags. The collar was pearlescent pink with rhinestones that dazzled in the moonlight. The tag declared the dog's name, *Lucy,* in a fancy calligraphy font.

Aaliyah highly doubted there were any E.C.C.O. agents running around with Lucy. She flipped over the tag and found an address. This was the Yancey's dog! Funny, they hadn't mentioned one.

She didn't want to leave Lucy alone, or be followed by her, so she wrote a note and attached it to Lucy's collar. It said, *'Had to leave unexpectedly due to a family emergency. Please watch Lucy for us! Thank you, the Yanceys.'* She tied the dog to the neighbors' porch.

As she walked away, Lucy began to bark after her and the noise caused the neighbors to turn on their lights and investigate. Aaliyah, hiding in the bushes at the edge of the treeline, was relieved when they happily took Lucy into their home. *Thank God they are dog lovers,* she sighed to herself.

She had continued on and found her way to the old church once again. One of the volunteers there led her into a basement where she could be hidden away and not be asked to have her chip scanned before receiving food rations.

The main organized religions in the country had either been forced out or oppressed into submission by E.C.C.O. The few stragglers remaining had formed underground cooperative groups that were connected to the Guardian.

The freedom of religion was only one of the many freedoms taken away by E.C.C.O., but its loss had left a gaping hole in the society that remained.

The Guardian didn't espouse any specific religion, but reached out to anyone who was suffering under the current authorities' abuses. The whole ship was comprised of victims the current system had either persecuted outwardly or ignored purposefully. Aaliyah had witnessed firsthand how the Guardian provided a place for the abused and broken to begin again.

As she was deep in thought, a slender woman of Asian ancestry came and sat by Aaliyah. Her clothes were mismatched and she looked malnourished, pale and weak. She smiled slightly before she bowed her head humbly in silent prayer.

They both sat eating their soup at an otherwise empty table. Aaliyah woke from her thoughts and looked over at the woman.

"My name's Aaliyah."

The slight woman nodded her head and took another spoonful of soup. She swallowed and then said in a whisper, "Call me Elizabeth."

Aaliyah didn't know if it was her real name or not, but was leaning towards the likelihood that it was not. She understood. Getting caught here by E.C.C.O. meant trouble and trust was a luxury most could not afford.

She began to regret giving out her real name. *Had she been too careless?*

"Have you been here long?" Aaliyah dared to ask. She was trying to get a sense of whether she could trust her or not. Her answer was shocking.

The woman shook her head and whispering, she declared, "I came here to find you."

Fear seeped out of Aaliyah's pores. She subconsciously held her breath. The woman's face was unwavering.

"I have a message for you from the Guardian."

She pulled out a manila envelope from her knapsack. After Aaliyah took it from her, she smiled and said, "Godspeed!"

She rose and left Aaliyah staring at the envelope in her hand. It amazed her the Guardian could know exactly where she was and get a message to her so quickly! The Guardian was truly extraordinary.

There were two smaller envelopes inside. Aaliyah opened the one addressed to her. After opening it, she unfolded colorful origami paper to uncover a hand written message scrawled across the plain white side.

"Go to these addresses in the order given. They will be your safe houses until you complete this mission. You are to rescue this man (a picture of a demure man in a gray suit was pasted there) His name is Stanley Reynolds. Please give him the second letter and ask him to come with you. You must both return to the ship. Also, memorize this phrase "Biun chung mu ji" You will need it in the future.

In unarmed truth and unconditional love,
The Guardian."

Ten addresses were listed on the bottom of the page. Aaliyah read over the odd phrase she was told to remember. *What language was that?* It sounded like gibberish coming out of her mouth.

But one thing the Guardian had written was very familiar to her. The Guardian had quoted from one of Aaliyah's heroes, the forgotten civil rights leader, Martin Luther King, Jr.

Aaliyah had the complete quote written in a notebook on the nightstand in her cabin aboard *The Remnant*. It was a well-worn biography of him given to her by a volunteer at the church the first time she had hidden out there. She had never really taken the time to read it until she had boarded *The Remnant*. The inspiring words of the Reverend Martin Luther King, Jr. had become very familiar to her over the last few years. These she had memorized…

"I believe that unarmed truth and unconditional love will have the final word in reality. This is why right, temporarily defeated, is stronger than evil triumphant."

Aaliyah stood up and searched the room for the mysterious woman who had given her the note, but she had disappeared.

The first address was on the south side of the city. There was no way she could risk driving a car since she had no way to purchase gas. Even if she could, cars were rare.

Since bicycles were fairly common, she could blend in better on two wheels. She asked the volunteers if they could hook her up with a bike. Someone had left one behind years ago, a blue Trek. After it had been tuned up and they provided her with a repair kit, spare tubes, a portable tire pump and some cycling shorts, Aaliyah was ready.

After a shower and a full night's sleep, Aaliyah donned her backpack, filled the bike's pannier with packaged food, water and limited toiletries, mounted the bike and pedaled away with the rising sun on her left side.

Her journey was long and tiring on the old bicycle. She took a few days off to rest, but on the days she rode, she covered anywhere from sixty to eighty kilometers a day, filling up the tires with the old hand pump and lubing the chain regularly.

Because of E.C.C.O.'s restrictions on vehicles, the roads were almost deserted, and in bad disrepair. She passed more bikes than cars. No one gave her a second glance.

The addresses she had been given were sometimes residences, sometimes abandoned churches with shelters in their basements, sometimes a business that had a Guardian-friendly owner. She was always expected and always provided for. But the rigid bicycle seat wore out her backside and she was constantly in fear of being stopped by agents. *Abundant life,* Aaliyah reminded herself, laughing about the irony. Two weeks later, she arrived at the last preordered address, the final safe house, and received her final instructions.

***

Reynolds awoke in the room he had been residing in since joining up with the doctor again. He immediately felt lighter emotionally. The fog had cleared. Most importantly- he was alive! The mad doctor hadn't killed him after all!

He now realized how very much he wanted to live. *How could he have risked his life like that?* He had obviously been severely disturbed.

There was a knock on the door. Reynolds instinctively replied "*Jin!*"

Dr. Griffin strode in, his handsome strong-jawed face full of pride. He looked Reynolds up and down.

"How do you feel?"

Reynolds did not smile, but simply answered truthfully, "Good."

The doctor chuckled. He needed Reynolds to be healthy again. He was the only one he could trust and there was more to be done.

The doctor asked Reynolds to go out to pick up a delivery and then go to the local market to buy some supplies. It appeared he was back to being the doctor's errand boy.

He downloaded the list to his Com and went down to the garage to find the doctor's vehicle. He was once quite the driver, but the city's driving ordinances over the past twenty years had kept him from driving anything other than an occasional limousine.

He walked up to the bright yellow sports car with trepidation. After performing a few jerky starts, grinding into second gear and overcoming a tendency to over-steer, he found himself once again quite comfortable behind the wheel. He mastered the manual shifting and made good use of the sticky tires. Driving this powerful car on the open road in the countryside was...a thrill.

He arrived at the delivery service center. The boxes he loaded into the small trunk of the car were about the size of a cereal box. There were six of them and they all had "bio-hazard" and "flammable material" warning signs. He loaded them carefully into the small trunk and continued on to the market.

The list on his Com was all out of order. Groceries and toiletries were jumbled interchangeably. Reynolds found himself wandering the isles hunting down one thing only to return to the same isle five minutes later.

As he made his way down isle 10 for the tenth time, it seemed, he began to have the feeling he was being watched.

No doubt, his shopping strategies could be considered entertaining to some, but at that moment, it wasn't his shopping skills that were being scrutinized- it was his face.

***

Aaliyah was sure. Well, about 90% sure, anyway. He was wearing a gray, nondescript suit, even on this unusually hot day, and his long horse face seemed to be a very close match to the one on the picture before her.

She followed him covertly as he made his way to the checkout counter.

On his way out to the parking lot, Reynolds felt paranoid. *Was it a side effect of the ECT procedure?* After he closed the trunk and sidled onto the cushioned driver's seat, he noticed an envelope on the passenger side seat. The lone word handwritten on the front was 'Stanley.'

No one ever referred to him only as 'Stanley.' No one except...*her.*

He uncharacteristically ripped open the envelope and began to read the note. His eyes turned into saucers. He read it three times, each time out of increasing disbelief. After the fourth read-through, he set it down, got out of the car, and looked around.

Was she here? Could she see him now? He jumped as a voice behind him asked,

"Are you Stanley Reynolds?"

He turned to find a self-assured, dark-skinned woman staring at him. He cleared his throat and replied, "Yes."

There was nothing else to add. He was Stanley Reynolds.

"I've come to rescue you," she said bluntly. Reynolds was taken aback.

"Rescue me? From what?"

"That's not my department. I am only following my orders."

"Your orders? Who do you work for? E.C.C.O.?"

"No, Mr. Suit. Not anymore."

Aaliyah stepped closer to Reynolds and spoke in hushed tones.

"I work for the Guardian and I was assigned to rescue you. I need to take you to our ship." She glanced around, hoping no one was listening in to their conversation.

"What ship? What are you-"

He was cut off by the sound of his Com beeping. He saw the caller and knew better than to make him wait.

"*Da fu!* Yes, Doctor?"

Aaliyah impatiently waited, listening to the one-sided conversation with growing restlessness. As the man in the suit said, "*Wan bi!*" she decided to interject, only to discover he was now finished with his call.

"Sorry, ma'am, you're going to have to rescue me later, I have to get back now."

"Excuse me?" she replied, her voice thick with attitude. She threw him an accompanying attitude-laced glare.

"If I don't return, my boss will *really* kill me this time, ma'am," he spoke with a matter-of-fact tone.

"If you don't come with me, you might wish he had!" she retorted, "And stop calling me 'ma'am'!

"Didn't you read what was in that envelope? I'm not going to pretend I know what it said, 'cause I don't invade others' privacy, but I figure it was something pretty important!

Someone gave me that letter to deliver to you personally. You must be pretty special, Mr. Suit!

"Now, c'mon, let's go! We can take your car," she said, opening the passenger side door and sitting down. She slammed the door shut and buckled up.

Reynolds just stood there, staring at this complete stranger. She was probably the boldest woman he had ever seen. *What should I do?* The letter was mind-blowing enough. Now he had to deal with this strange lady and her crazy insistence on "rescuing" him?

The letter. *The letter... It was from Olivia.* She was alive and she remembered him! His heart fluttered as he thought about her. Maybe this audacious woman could take her to see Olivia.

The thought of seeing her again gave him courage.

Besides, he had survived the procedure. More than ever before, he wanted to live in freedom.

If he continued working for Dr. Griffin, he would never be free. This was his best chance. Reynolds threw his Com across the parking lot, got in the blazing yellow vehicle and spun out of the parking lot like a professional race car driver.

He was smiling the whole time.

18 The Stranger

Ellen had checked on Li and there was no change. His fever was held at bay with interchanging doses of ibuprofen and acetaminophen, but kept returning. Connor Reid had agreed to stay by his side and let her know when his fever broke. The ocean water and the coldness had been a debilitating combination and he had succumbed to some kind of virus.

The fever was the worst of it. It was causing Li to have febrile dreams in which he would cry out for Ainsling or for his long-lost mother. Ellen's heart broke as she thought about how neither of them were there to answer his cries.

It was up to his friends on board *The Remnant* to nurse him back to health. Mark Yancey had stopped by to check on him a few times, once with Lisa and once with the Captain. Pastor Dave visited him, praying out loud over him. The Captain came twice a day and read to him from his collection of poetry, pulling out his favorites for him.

On the third day of his fever, the Captain was reading some Walt Whitman when Li began to wake.

"'…I am not to speak to you,
I am to think of you when I sit alone or wake at night alone,
I am to wait, I do not doubt I am to meet you again,
I am to see to it that I do not lose you.'"

The Captain finished the poem entitled "The Stranger," and closed the book. He looked at Li and noticed his head moving. His eyelids fluttered. They closed and then opened wide. He turned his head towards the Captain and whispered, "Don't leave."

The Captain smiled.

"How are you, son?"

"I feel like crap- you?"

"It's been a long couple of days. You've had us all worried." He set the old book down on the night stand.

"Sorry," Li replied, "I don't usually get sick. How's the new rescue? Did he get sick, too?"

"No, but I gave him his own cabin. He said you snore."

Li was too tired to roll his eyes. The Captain reached for his cane. Li watched him struggle to stand up and asked,

"How come you've never told me about what happened to your leg? I got nothing but time now."

"Not much to tell. Car accident." He shrugged. Li sat up a little. "That's it? Seriously? C'mon!"

Li was hoping for more. The Captain's face was stoic under his beard. He grimaced as he obviously ignored Li's plea for a detailed description of his injury and pursued a change of subject matter.

"You better rest up. I'll get Ellen- she wanted us to tell her the minute your fever broke. She's like a mama hen when it comes to you young folk. She won't even give me a cough drop."

The Captain closed the door as he left. The hall was quiet. Prodded by Li's inquiry, he couldn't help but to think back on the accident that had caused his limp. That fateful incident had proven both a tragedy and a miracle.

It was ten years ago. Once again, he was headed to the docks to do maintenance on his boat, *The St. Augustine.* Out of nowhere, a small child raced out into the street and directly into the path of his car. He later discovered the child had been chasing an errant ball. In his failed attempt to avoid hitting the child he swerved and crashed into a tree.

The next thing he knew, he was waking up in the hospital and learned he had permanently damaged his knee. It was terrible news, but not as terrible as what they told him next. The child, a five-year-old boy named Jordan, was in a coma.

It had all happened so fast. He thought he had avoided hitting him, but the rear end of his car had fish-tailed and swept into the small boy, throwing him into the air.

The authorities labeled it an accident. But he never forgot that child's face.

He decided to sell his boat after that. All his love for it had been washed away on that fateful day. His boat was now only a big, painful reminder of how his negligence had taken away that child's future.

Two months later, he went to the docks to meet an interested buyer for his boat. The child was still in a coma and he could never forgive himself. As a neuroscientist, he knew well the chances of the child walking up from the coma were slim. The severe injury to his knee didn't feel like enough punishment.

As he limped along the boardwalk, he located the restaurant they had agreed to meet at. He was told to look for a woman with long, black hair wearing a red hat. Though it was mysterious, he was grateful not to have to ask at the restaurant for her or wobble around searching for her on the new cane he wasn't used to using yet.

As she turned around and reached out her hand to shake his, he had a sense of familiarity towards her. It was as if they were already acquainted, but he couldn't place her face.

After selling his old boat to her, she surprised him by offering him an opportunity. She was a wealthy businesswoman and wanted to buy a fleet of old cruise ships. She wondered if he would like to be the Captain on one of her ships.

He asked her, "Why me?"

To which she replied, "I believe you are the right one for the job."

By the time the fleet was purchased and all the paperwork was completed, E.C.C.O. had been voted in and freedoms started to disappear. The division of the country into Sectors and the introduction of the chip were the first major changes. John had a chip imbedded in his hand just like everyone else.

His new employer called him to schedule his first day onboard his new ship. He met with her and the crew. She introduced each employee with a note of compassion in her voice, which was an atypical gesture for someone with so much authority.

As he got to know each of them, he discovered their stories all had a similar thread. Each person gathered there had a legacy of sordid lives, unfortunate circumstances, or various sins they had committed. Despite this, they were each offered a job.

After a few months, John concluded this was a ship manned by losers, of which he considered himself the biggest one. After a year of leading tour groups around the bay, taking rich tourists out to see the sights, their unique boss came personally to the ship and announced a change in the target market.

"E.C.C.O. has begun to access people's worthiness," she informed them, "They are beginning to pronounce some people 'unproductive.' This type of governance is not new. It has happened many times throughout history. My friends, the outcasts of society will suffer greatly. All of you know what it feels like to suffer, in some form or fashion. More importantly, you know how it feels to be rescued. I am asking you to join me in rescuing the outcasts. Together we can keep hope alive."

She then explained her outrageous plan to them, putting herself at risk of being reported by any one of them to E.C.C.O.

What she proposed would be illegal. But it was right. And they all knew it. Every one of them had their chip removed and dedicated their lives to this new venture- the great rescue.

That was the beginning of John Capitani's new life aboard the ship they had christened *The Remnant*. He was now a veteran in the rescue business.

The Captain opened the door and entered his suite. Connor Reid looked up from his card game with his newly reunited daughter, Ainsling, and gave him a nod. Ainsling shyly hid behind her fan of cards, desperate to avoid eye contact with the Captain.

"Connor, could you find Ellen and take her to Li? He has woken up and it appears his fever has broken." Connor and Ainsling looked at each other and he squeezed her hand in reassurance. Without a word, he left to search for Ellen.

"I don't suppose you want to see him?" the Captain asked Ainsling. "You know he called out your name many times. He has been worried about you for quite a long time."

"I'm not the same girl he once knew. Let him be happy without me." She hung her head and her hand wandered to her ankle, where there was something missing.

"I don't know why you haven't made me walk the plank or whatever. I expect you to. I'm a spy, after all! E.C.C.O. might arrest you anytime now, and it's...it's all my fault!"

It had been days since her report on Lisa. She had vengefully given Lisa's name to Dr. Griffin and she had no doubt that he had relayed the information to his contacts at E.C.C.O. They would surely track her to the ship.

"Why haven't you forced her to remove her chip? Then you would be safe," she told him.

"We are big on extending grace here on *The Remnant*. So, we don't force people to join us. We rescue- they decide. She has been given three additional days to make her choice."

He seemed remarkably unconcerned.

"How have your reports been going?"

She shrugged.

"He seems to be getting irritated. I haven't given him any juicy information lately."

"Tell me more about how you trigger the device," he said, changing the subject.

"Well, I must think about something that makes me feel… well, *miserable,* I guess. It can be anger, fear, or sadness. Not just a little bit, but a *lot* of anger or fear. If those feelings go away, it shuts off and I become visible again."

She watched him fill up a kettle with bottled water.

"I can extend the cloak to cover other things, too. But if I cloak another person, it does something bad to them."

"What do you mean?" he asked.

She remembered poor Mr. Reynolds and wondered if he had ever recovered. He had been quite unhinged the last time she saw him. Ugh. Now she had more guilt to add to her already full tank.

"People, unlike objects, seem to feel my feelings *with* me when I cloak them. It affects their brain in a bad way, I guess."

She didn't fully understand it herself, so it was hard to explain.

The Captain continued to gather information. She had told him a little about the device when she had first been discovered, but he needed to learn more. He needed to know how far Griffin had gone. And if there was hope of reversing the damage done.

"And you no longer have seizures?" He landed the tea kettle on the hotplate.

"No," she replied. Griffin had kept his promise concerning her seizures. Of course, he had also promised to make her a butterfly. What she had become now was far from that.

"What about that contraption around his wrist you told me about before? How does that work?"

He watched the kettle impatiently, as if he could hurry up the heating process with his glare, which goes against the old saying about a watched pot never boiling. His glare was unrelated to culinary endeavors. Hearing about this sadistic, twisted function of Griffin's device made him simmer with anger.

"Sorry, I don't really know how it works. He pushes some buttons together and it makes my body hurt all over. Every fiber of my being hurts! He can even use it on me here, and who knows how many miles away he is! It *seriously* hurts," she emphasized, shaking at the mere memory of those electric jolts coursing through her.

"I'm sorry this happened to you. I once suspected Jay was responsible for some terrible things, but there was never enough proof. I certainly never envisioned he would do *this*.

Unfortunately, he will probably be revered as a genius now instead of the madman he truly is. His time has come."

The Captain lamented the day E.C.C.O. had come to power. Their new categorization of society negated the ethics of scientific research. Scientists were free to use those deemed "unproductive" in all kinds of unimaginable experiments without any restrictions.

Jay Griffin had done what no scientist would have been allowed to do twenty years ago. His overarching advantage was the secrecy of his project. Yet, even if someone blew the whistle on him, he wouldn't be stopped. He would just have the glory of it taken from him.

Interrupting the Captain's thoughts, the kettle finally whistled. He turned off the heat and lifted it. As he poured the steaming water, Ainsling thought of some questions for him.

"So, if the Guardian rescued Li, why didn't I get rescued too?"

She was despondent. *Why rescue only Li? I was the one who was going to be changed into a monster. He was normal. It wasn't fair!*

"The Guardian isn't the only one with plans. We had planned to rescue you; then, Jay rushed your surgery and we never got the chance. But look- here you are!" he proclaimed, throwing out his arms towards her.

She grimaced.

"I don't think your Guardian knows what he's doing."

"Do you think the Guardian works for you alone? You may need to change your perspective. For instance, what if you considered the device a gift?" Ainsling's eyes widened at him, appalled.

"No way!" she exclaimed.

"Ah, don't be so quick to decide. *'What you had planned for evil, God had planned for good.'*"

He quoted from the biblical tale of Joseph, a faithful man whose life was changed dramatically by betrayal and redemption. It had always been one of his favorites. Somehow Ainsling's situation had brought it to mind.

Before Ainsling could interject and tell him what she really thought about any God who would allow this to happen to her, he continued,

"From the beginning, man has been trying to replace God. We think we know better! As if!" He had a twinkle in his eye, finding that idea amusing somehow.

"Li told me about your red string theory," he added.

"It's not a 'theory', it's-"

She stopped. *Why explain it? It didn't matter anymore.*

"What? He gave me the impression it was important to you. It is to him. Whatever Griffin told you about Li was a lie, Ainsling! Haven't you noticed that bright red string tied around his ankle?"

She hadn't. Her heart suddenly sank, weighing her down.

"You may have given up on yourself, but there are those of us who refuse to do so. I think you would be wise to join us."

Hope struggled to invade the room, even Ainsling could sense it, though it was invisible and blocked by fear. The Captain rested the sugar bowl in front of her mug of tea. He smiled a wise, fatherly smile.

"Ainsling, we have all been in need of a rescue. Don't dismiss this chance so easily."

He spoke as if he had experience in the matter. She wondered what he could possibly have gone through that could compare to this. Whatever he had experienced, it couldn't have been this bad. He was still alive, even free-and in charge of this ship!

If she hadn't been reunited with her father, Ainsling would have willingly walked the plank. She would have run off it! She certainly deserved it. But it would hurt her father too much.

She was tempted to give in, to let go. But the guilt of what she had done was too much.

"I almost killed Lisa. I don't deserve another chance."

"Yeah, you don't. Remember what I said about being big on grace here? If you *deserved* another chance, it wouldn't be *grace*. Grace is just the beginning though. I think this author sums it up nicely…"

He pulled a book off the shelf and flipped through the pages until he found what he was looking for. It was a book by Anne Lamott. He handed it to Ainsling and insisted that she read aloud the highlighted sentence.

"I do not understand at all the mystery of grace- only that it meets us where we are but does not leave us where it found us."

"Grace is a catalyst for change, to use scientific jargon," the Captain explained.

"Being rescued is only the beginning. Being redeemed is the real journey."

"You make grace sound pretty amazing," she responded.

*Amazing Grace…*It had been a long time since that song had played in Sector One.

Ainsling thought about this. She agreed that she certainly didn't deserve anything she had now. The Captain should have kicked her off of this ship after he found out what a monster she was. Instead, he offered her a place to live with the father she had once believed was dead.

But she was no longer a naïve little girl. Reality had slapped her into submission. *Sometimes dreams turn on you.* The device in her brain was evidence of that. Her cure was now her curse.

Could grace really do anything about that?

19 The Road Trip

"I don't care how busy you are, find him!"

Dr. Griffin slammed his Com down and growled through his teeth. *Where could that imbecile be?* he thought. *And all my supplies!*

He slammed his fist onto the lab table. The beakers shook and made an irreverently happy tinkling sound. He had been ready to produce more serum, just as he had promised his benefactors.

If he didn't locate Reynolds and his supplies in the next few days, he would have to make up some excuse and stall as he located more of the rare ingredients for his unique serum. That would make him lose face. He couldn't allow himself to be belittled by his benefactors. Why hadn't he put a retribution device on Reynolds? He had an overwhelming desire to make him hurt right now.

His connections at E.C.C.O. were supposed to be good at tracking people through their chips. He wondered if they had made any progress on locating Lisa Yancey and that ship of John Capitani's.

Good old John... He could never abide that pathetic pseudo-scientist philosopher. It was degrading to have been the underling of that man at the Institute. Many of the other scientists there laughed at John Capitani and his mock science behind his back. It had been humiliating to have been fired from the Institute by him.

On second thought, he should actually thank him for that. Little did that religious nut know it was the best thing that could have happened to him! His connections and those who funded his research provided him with a new space and some new challenges. Most of those connections soon found themselves in high places under E.C.C.O.

He kept his research and progress secret, not because he was scared of the authorities, but because he knew that being the sole bearer of this knowledge gave him power- power that could not easily be taken or demoted. He alone knew how to create this device and the serum used to produce the cloaking capability. His benefactors were counting on his skills. His alone.

Now he had made the mistake of trusting another person. He thought Reynolds would be grateful to him for curing his condition. After all the years he had known the man, he had only once been unreliable. That was years ago, and Reynolds had proven all the more reliable afterwards.

The fact he was missing was quite a puzzle. Reynolds must have been attacked and lying in a ditch somewhere.

Maybe he ran away? Nah! He had a hard time imagining Reynolds being man enough to risk joyriding away in his new sports car.

Whatever had happened to Reynolds, he needed to find out before his supplies were ruined!

***

"You don't have to drive so *fast!*" Aaliyah yelled at the stiffly dressed man behind the wheel.

Reynolds hadn't realized he had been going so fast. With the road clear and open, it was hard to suppress the inner racer inside him. Driving gave him an exhilarated feeling. That, and the letter from Olivia, made him…happy.

"I'm sorry, ma'am. I thought you were in a hurry to get to your ship," he said, lifting his foot off the pedal slightly.

He could see her muscles relax a bit. She was a striking woman- strong, confident, if not somewhat bossy, with a well-defined bone structure and heart-shaped brick red lips.

"Stop staring at me, Suit! Keep your eyes on the road! We are in a hurry, but I'd prefer to get there in one piece!"

She set her jaw and gave him an awkward look. "It took me two whole weeks to get here by bicycle from the city. It'll take about six hours to drive back. Hope you're up for a little road trip, Fancypants!"

She leaned back in her chair. Her bottom was still pretty sore, and her legs were so tired. She was about to close her eyes when she felt him staring at her again.

"I said to stop staring at me! For your information, I have a third-degree black belt in Tae Kwon Do, so don't you go getting any funny ideas! I'll kick you into the middle of next week, along with that nice suit of yours!" Her expression was so animated when she talked Reynolds almost smiled while she was yelling at him.

He actually *felt* like smiling! His newfound freedom, mixed with the excitement of receiving Olivia's letter and the adventure before him, was transforming him into... a man who smiled.

He cleared his throat, turned his eyes back on the road, and replied, "Yes, ma'am."

"Ugh. Stop calling me that. My name is Aaliyah. Ah-*lee*-yah," she pronounced it for him.

"Well, Aaliyah, my name is Stanley," he paused. "Not 'Mr. Suit.' And I'm sorry for staring. It's just that you are…unique."

Aaliyah didn't know how to respond for once. She smiled shyly and tipped her head to him,

"Nice to meet you. Do you mind if I call you 'Stan?' You look more like a 'Stan' than a 'Stanley' to me. 'Stanley' is a grandpa-sounding name. You're my age, aren't you?"

No one had ever asked him such a personal question before.

"I'm forty-five," he responded. She raised her eyebrows.

"Really? I'm thirty-eight. Can you tell?"

"You can't be *that* old!" he blurted out.

She burst out in laughter.

"You don't socialize much, do you?"

"No, ma- I mean, *Aaliyah*, I don't. I work a lot," he explained. She smiled. Her white teeth were stunning behind her full, dark lips.

They spent the next six hours talking. Reynolds had never spent that much time in conversation. He found himself saying things he'd only thought before, but never verbalized. Aaliyah listened to his ramblings as if his words were the most important ones ever spoken.

He found himself smiling, even chuckling, at some of the stories she told him about life on the ship. She could be very serious, he discovered, but her manner could change as quick as lightening and she would be joking again.

They stopped to eat and he bought them a couple cups of coffee for the long drive ahead. He placed the coffee in the cup holders and waited in the car for her to return from the bathroom. She seemed to be taking a long time, and he began to wonder if she was okay. He got out of the car, locked the doors, and walked back towards the restaurant.

There she was, sitting at a booth inside, a glass in her hand, leaning back in the booth. Two men in the booth behind her rose and went to the register to pay. She quickly sidled out the door behind their backs.

She glimpsed Stan walking towards her and waved at him to go back to the car. He just stood there, confused. She rushed over to him.

"Get in the car Stan! *Hurry!*"

She grabbed his arm and started to run with him. They rushed into the car, Aaliyah looking franticly at the disappearing door of the restaurant behind them.

"Stan- *drive fast*- now!"

He stomped on the gas pedal and about a mile down the road, he asked, "What happened?"

"Just keep driving fast. Let me ask you one thing. It's important, okay?"

He pushed down on the pedal a little more, shifted gears and waited for her question.

"Are you glad to be rescued?" She knew this was bad timing, but she had no choice now.

"Y-yes, yes I am!" he replied quickly, sensing the panic in her voice.

"You know the Guardian sent me to rescue you. I hate to be so direct, but if we don't get that chip out of your hand now, the two agents I overheard back at that diner are going to track us down and all will be lost! Are you willing to do it, Stan? Normally we give people more time to think it over, but we're running out of time!"

She had to explain quickly. The agents following them were trained in their own kind of rescue and it would not be a pleasant experience.

Aaliyah had been having, well, a nice time, amazingly, with Stan up till then. This was an unfortunate turn of events. She waited anxiously for his answer.

"I'll do it!" he said confidently. He could hardly wait to be free from Dr. Griffin for good. He felt quite stupid for not thinking about the chip before now.

"Do you have a knife?"

She did, but he couldn't drive and get his hand cut open all at the same time. He pulled into the back of a gas station they saw ahead on the highway. She sanitized her small switchblade with an alcohol swab from a first-aid kit and Aaliyah proceeded to make a parallel incision to the original on his palm and, as quickly as possible, pulled out the tiny chip that was being used to track their position.

Stan gritted his teeth through the procedure. Aaliyah found a band aid in the kit and also wrapped his hand with gauze so he could drive without too much discomfort.

Then Aaliyah had an idea.

They grabbed their bags, along with the supplies from the trunk, and waited. They ran over to another car while the owner went inside to use the facilities or shop or whatever and drove off in their vehicle.

When the owner came back out and saw his car was gone, he looked around for it. On the gas pump, there was a string attached to a set of keys with a note.

The note said, "A present from the Guardian."

***

Dr. Griffin held the hastily scribbled note in his hand. *The Guardian, huh?*

The agent had returned his car. It had been located almost ten hours after his last Com call with Reynolds. They had found Stanley Reynolds' bloody chip stuck between the passenger seat cushions.

After searching the car himself, he was beyond angry. The delivery Reynolds had picked up was missing. And now he had no way to find it!

20 The Reunion

"Ainsling, this has been an *extremely bad* day. So there's no new information? No new 'rescues'- or whatever they call them?"

Dr. Griffin didn't really care, but preferred to have something to record that would show his benefactors the value of his unique device.

This included information and actions one couldn't get or accomplish without the cloaking ability. For example, the tricks Ainsling had played on that Lisa girl. That still made him smile.

"No more pranks? Feel free to experiment a little- just don't get caught, or you will be sentencing them all to death. I know what a humanitarian you are. You don't want anyone to die because of you, do you?" he asked her snidely.

She frowned and replied, "No, Dr. Griffin."

Ainsling wondered how he planned on getting her back. She had been dropped off at the bar where Mark Yancey frequented and told to stay with him no matter what happened. She had no idea where she was- or how to get back on shore.

The only happiness she had found on the ship was with her father. Yet she was desperate to leave. He wouldn't understand, but she knew he was better off without her.

She whole-heartedly hated Dr. Griffin, but she accepted it was inevitable she would have to return to him someday. *But how? And when?* These questions plagued her.

Ainsling was unable to be tracked by any means. It was one of the strengths of the device. Being cloaked wouldn't be an advantage if you could be discovered electronically or digitally. Thermal imaging didn't work on her, either, because her body temperature dropped when cloaked.

Never being implanted with a chip made her untraceable also. She didn't have the nerve to ask if E.C.C.O. had tracked Lisa's chip yet. The memory of the pain from the retribution band kept her from asking questions that would annoy him. He had already said he was having a bad day.

Interrupting her thoughts, Dr. Griffin's irritated voice spit out of the Com,

"Ainsling? Did you hear me? I said to remember to stay away from Li. He's only interested in himself. All he can give you is trouble!"

"Yes, Dr. Griffin. I am all alone here, don't worry. Li is busy working for the Guardian and the Captain. I never see him, anyway."

There was a pregnant pause. Then, the doctor's voice came through the Com, "Did you say the Guardian?"

"Yes, that's what the people on this ship are here for- to follow this Guardian person. That's who tells them who to rescue and when. I told you about this before."

"Yes, yes, I remember now!"

"I need some sleep, Dr. Griffin. Is there anything else you want to know?"

"No, you have been very informative, Ainsling. One more thing- report *promptly* at 11:30 tomorrow! *Wan bi!*"

Ainsling set down her Com. All was now quiet in the small cabin she shared with her father. He was asleep.

Since being reunited with him, she hadn't risked cloaking again. The Captain had recommended taking a break to regain emotional control anyway. But no amount of control could wash away the tremendous guilt over the things she had done.

The Captain went on and on about mercy, compassion, and grace. All that talk about grace was overwhelming. She wanted to be punished, not forgiven. *Why didn't anyone understand?*

Li was out of danger, but was confined to his room. She was relieved to hear he was healthy again. Her father told her about how Li had jumped into the cold ocean to save him from drowning.

He was a good boy. She'd always known that. Dr. Griffin didn't know him at all. Life aboard this ship, along with its revolutionary crew, must have brought out his strengths.

Her heart ached. She must avoid seeing him once he was up and about again. Not because of Griffin's orders. But because, for now, that was all the punishment she would get. It was temporarily sufficient.

The Reid's room was across the hall from the Captain's. Ainsling wondered if the Captain was still awake. She opened her door a crack and peered out into the hall. No one. She exited it quietly and walked across the small hallway to knock on the Captain's door.

As she was about to knock, the door opened.

Li stood there.

He looked at her standing there before him and blinked hard. He shook his head as if to wake himself up. Then he rubbed the back of his neck.

Ainsling tried to will her feet to move, to run, but they weren't obeying. She hadn't triggered the device, not because the Captain had recommended that she refrain from doing so for as long as possible in order to stabilize her mental state, but because she was simply in shock.

"Li, what's wrong?"

The Captain hobbled up behind him and looked over Li's shoulder. "I see," he said.

Li continued to stare at her and did not move out of the doorway. Ainsling's feet felt glued to the floor. Time seemed stuck in place as well.

"Why don't you both come in? There is much to say and the time to say it is *now,* okay, Ainsling?"

Li stepped backwards slowly; still staring at the apparition the Captain had just addressed as 'Ainsling.'

The ghost before him frowned. Her pale face was identical to the one from his dream that night he sat at Mr. Yancey's bedside. Yet this time he wasn't the only one seeing his dream.

The Captain pulled out a chair and motioned for her to sit in it. The ghost-girl sat, looking quite anxious. He wanted to reach out and touch her hand to see if she was indeed made of flesh.

The waif-like girl looked at the floor, drawing breath purposefully and slowly.

He had to know!

He reached out and grasped her hand, not expecting to actually feel its existence under his. Yet there was soft skin, and warmth. Warmth proved her humanity. She was not a ghost!

"You're the girl from my dream," he spoke in a whisper. Then with more volume, he asked, "Are you *really* Ainsling?"

The Captain set glasses of water in front of them and spoke to Li.

"She wouldn't let me tell you she was here. She seems to have lost faith in the red string. Maybe you can set her straight. She won't listen to this old man."

The Captain turned to Ainsling and pleaded, "Tell him everything. Remember what I said about grace. It's only amazing if you give it a chance." He hobbled over to the cabin door and left.

The two long-lost friends sat in silence for a few minutes, until Li asked, "Where have you been?"

"I don't know where he took me. Dr. Griffin performed my surgery earlier than planned. It was right after you left me. Afterwards we moved around a lot." She paused, having difficulty transforming her thoughts into words. He patiently listened as she forced the words out of her mouth.

"Li, you need to know something. He *changed* me." She hesitated, standing up and turning away from him. She didn't want to see his face as she spoke the next line,

"I am different now."

"What do you mean?"

"He put a device in my head that cured my seizures, but it gave me a special ability, too."

"A special ability?"

"It's a cloaking device. I can become…invisible," she informed him, waiting to hear words of disbelief, or even laughter.

"So that's what the big deal was! He was never so excited about anything before, I knew it must be big, but- *wow!* That is… amazing!"

When she turned away and didn't respond, he reconsidered. "Except- it's not, huh?"

Li's handsome face switched from displaying awe to showing sympathy. Ainsling turned around and studied him, trying to decide if she should go on. She was shocked that he appeared to care about her. *Why?*

'He doesn't get it,' she rationalized. The Captain was right. She needed to tell him everything.

"Um, no, it's not… amazing for me. The device is implanted inside my brain, Li. To trigger the device, I have to focus on negative feelings, you know, like anger or pain. Using the cloak for long periods of time does something wonky to my brain. It's like I lose myself. I do things I shouldn't do. And your father has this band around his wrist he uses to hurt me if I don't do what he says.

"He ordered me to shadow Dr. Yancey and then to spy on this ship. This is my first mission. I'm a spy. He expects to impress some benefactor with his new invention. Are you following me?"

There was a deep undertone of despondency in her voice now. She stopped to consider her next words.

"The night you think you dreamt of me? It was real, Li. I had been cloaked for so long because I had to stay with Mr. Yancey- I hadn't learned how it would take control of my emotions. I said such mean things to you! I-I'm sorry." She had tears in her eyes.

"Sorry? You're sorry?"

Ainsling froze. She expected- even *wanted*- him to be angry with her, but it felt worse than she had imagined. Li went on,

"Ainsling, it sounds like my father's device doesn't let you think for yourself. What is there to forgive? It's not *your* fault! It's *his!*"

He wasn't angry at *her*, he was angry with his *father* for doing this to her! Suddenly he realized he had been fired simply to get him out of the way. That maniac! The anger he felt for his father now was unprecedented.

His temper cooled slightly when he saw Ainsling shaking nervously. She was conflicted because *he wasn't*. Despite everything, he was still on her side.

"Are you okay now? What can I do to help?"

At these words, she dropped to her knees, her forehead touching the floor, overwhelmed by his unexpected kindness.

She couldn't accept it. He didn't understand. He should hate her!

He rushed over to her and knelt down in front of her. He leaned over and pulled down the cuff of his sock, revealing the red string she had used to tie her final message to him, the one he found in his guitar.

"I never forgot you, Ainsling. We are tied together, right? I read the letter you left me. I don't know what to do yet, but I promise I will take care of you this time! I won't let my father take you away from me again!"

He reached his arms around her small, crumpled frame and held her tightly. She remained stiff and suffered her tears to fall silently.

Suddenly, she struggled vehemently, breaking free from his embrace, and stood up, backing away from him.

"Li, you don't know what I am capable of! Do you know what it's like to not feel anything but pain? I almost killed someone! You don't want to be tied to *me*. I'm a *monster!*"

Li was confused at her words and surprised at her strength.

"Look, Ainsling- you were the one who said the string could never break! I'm not going to stop caring about you just because you tell me to. It's too late for that! I never believed in anything or anyone until your crazy self came along and turned my life upside down. So don't think I'm gonna give up on you now!"

He stepped towards her and she defensively stepped back from him. His words were like water- hard to hold onto. He would change his mind once he had time to really understand what she told him.

She began to stagger backwards, away from him, towards the door. Without turning around, she said with finality,

"Let's pretend we never met. My father's alive and you are happy here. That's enough. I want you to live without me now- I'm not the Ainsling you used to know- immature and naïve. The red string is a *fairytale*, you idiot! Go on with your life! You belong here. But I- I will never be free like you. One day I'll have to leave. I have no choice. Goodbye, Li!"

She instantly vanished from his sight. He saw the door open and ran towards it, but she ran out into the hall, cloaked, and he didn't know which direction she had run.

"Ainsling!" he yelled over and over.

Li couldn't believe what she had said. *Pretend we never met? How could he do that? Arrgh!* He fought the urge to hit something or someone, just to get this overwhelming frustration out of him. Instead, he sank down to his knees right there in the hall and bowed his head low.

The Captain's voice played in his head, reciting the poem he had read at his bedside. *"I am to wait…I am to see to it that I do not lose you."*

Ellen and Pastor Dave were on their way back to their rooms when they saw Li crouched by the door of the Captain's cabin and decided to check if he was all right.

Pastor Dave slid his back down the wall and sat beside him. "What's up, Li?"

"I can't talk about it, Dave."

Dave and Ellen exchanged looks of sympathy and Dave laid his hand on Li's back and prayed a simple prayer. "Lord, give Li strength. Be his rock."

He stood up and said to Li, "Anytime you want to talk, I'm willing to listen."

"Me too, Li," said Ellen. "You don't have to suffer alone. Like we said from the beginning, we're on your side."

She squeezed his arm. He was too moved by their compassion to say anything. He slowly nodded his head in response. They respectfully left him alone until he was ready to talk.

Li was relieved by their concern. He decided to pray more. His initial desire to pound the wall was satiated as he did so. He held onto the red string adorning his ankle and decided there was only one thing he could do now- *wait*- just as the poet had written.

I won't lose her, Li thought.

21 The Punishment

"John, it's quite theoretical. You would need to see the PET scans and have a brilliant surgical team. I mean, it's not like Griffin's going to help you out," Yancey said negatively.

"I know. Even if I tried to explain it, I don't think he would be convinced a negative trigger is actually detrimental. The patient's mental health wouldn't be important enough for him to change his design. Besides, he would never listen to *me*. He never considered me to be a real scientist. *'Your observations are tainted by morals',* he used to say." John also looked discouraged.

"Jay is egomaniacal, John. He didn't have friends; he had *people*. If he couldn't use you, you were nothing to him."

That may have been true, but John Capitani didn't consider it helpful information. Jay was the only one who could tell them if, or how, they could alter the device.

"Is there anything we could use to ruin his reputation or something? You know, good old blackmail?" Mark asked in desperation.

Mark was finally thinking clearly again, but finding a solution for Ainsling's problem was beyond difficult. The girl was suffering due to this device and, as physicians, they naturally wanted to heal her- but there were a million obstacles to overcome. It would take a miracle.

"John, how is Li?" he wondered, moving on to another difficult problem.

"He is as determined as ever. Ainsling still refuses to see him. Her guilt is eating her up." He frowned. "I explained it all to Ellen and she suggested it would be best to wait for Ainsling to forgive herself and not to push her. Since Ellen has known her the longest, I trust her judgment. How is Lisa dealing with the unusual explanation of her injuries?"

John didn't expect Mark's proud daughter would deal with it gracefully.

"She made me explain it to her four times! I'm *still* not sure if she completely believes me. I can't say I blame her. I had a hard time with it myself. To think- Ainsling had been there with me that whole time!" He was red-faced with embarrassment.

Ellen knocked on the door and entered the suite, her eyes wide with excitement.

"Aaliyah has sent a message from shore! It came this morning with the supplies delivery!" They both perked up.

"She says she is safe. The Guardian sent her on a mission and she will be returning with a new rescue tomorrow!" Ellen related. She smiled heartily. It was good news indeed.

"Then we better get another cabin ready. Have someone give Aaliyah's room a fresh cleaning as well. Let's let her know how happy we are to have her back!" the Captain ordered. He beamed back at Ellen.

"I'll take care of it personally, Captain," Ellen replied and rushed out of the room.

The Captain sighed in relief. Aaliyah was safe! He had felt like he had lost an appendage after she insisted the rescue crew come back without her weeks ago. She was a vital and irreplaceable member of the ship and her missing presence had been hard to accept.

"Who's the new rescue?" Mark assumed John already knew.

"Do you think the Guardian tells *me* everything? We'll find out soon enough," he replied jokingly. There was another knock on his door.

"I'm popular today!" he exclaimed to Mark. "Come on in!"

Ainsling entered shyly, dragging her feet. She looked back and forth between the Captain and Mark Yancey. Mark tried to be friendly and welcoming, awkwardly giving her a forced smile. It seemed to have the opposite effect. She reacted to his smile like a cornered rabbit, looking for an escape.

"Ainsling, what can I do for you?" the Captain asked curiously.

She opened her mouth to speak, and then shut it as she disregarded her previous choice of wordage and considered others. Eventually, she declared simply, "I need to see Lisa."

Mark felt he should respond. "Why, Ainsling? I've already explained it to her."

"What did you explain? Did you tell her it 'wasn't really me'? Or that I have a 'special problem'? How did you explain away my actions?"

Ainsling had dropped her shy exterior and was being harshly blunt.

"You don't need to make excuses for me! I did what I *wanted* to do! It was still me, despite the device's influence. I take full responsibility!" Her eyes were full of indignation.

"Ainsling, I know you feel guilty, but-"

"I **am** guilty! I need to tell her- to confess face to face. It's the least I can do since no one else seems to see me for what I really am," she lowered her head again. It had become a habit now.

"If that's what you want, why don't you come with me and I'll show you to her room." Mark tried to comply. He honestly didn't blame her alone for what she had done. He only wished

Jay Griffin could have been stopped long ago. Hers wasn't the only life he had ruined.

Ainsling held out her hand to stop him- "I know where it is. Is she there now?"

When Mark affirmed she was, Ainsling left the room directly and the two men were left wondering how this confrontation would go. The two girls both had very strong personalities. Mark grew concerned. The word 'cat-fight' came to mind.

"Maybe we should go after her. Something bad might happen."

"And maybe it should. Let's let them try to work it out on their own first," John replied.

Ainsling marched resolutely to Lisa's cabin. She knocked on the door with a solid *tap-tap-tap*. The door was opened by a sister of Lisa's. Ainsling wanted to get this over with.

"May I speak to Lisa- *alone* please?"

"Lisa- some weird girl is here to talk to you- *alone!*"

Lisa suspiciously peeked from behind the door. Upon seeing her visitor, her face displayed a resigned acceptance.

"Yes?" she said shortly.

Ainsling remained determined, despite the other girl's understandable hatred towards her. It's not like she didn't deserve it.

"Can you step out?"

Lisa sidled into the hallway, closed the door of the cabin, and crossed her arms, wordlessly waiting for Ainsling to begin.

"I need to apologize to you. There isn't any way to make up for it, but I wanted you to know I am putting myself at your mercy. Anything you ask of me, I will do. It's all I can offer you for the wrongs I've done against you."

She looked straight into Lisa's eyes and Lisa could feel her sincerity. She seemed to *want* Lisa to punish her.

Lisa was speechless. This girl had read too many gothic novels or something. She thought for a while before responding,

"Can you leave the ship?"

"Not until I'm told to."

"*I'm* telling you! I thought you said I could ask you to do *anything?*" Lisa's voice was caustic.

"I *can't* leave until Dr. Griffin gets me out of here. I *want* to, Lisa, but I honestly *can't.*"

Griffin would punish her immensely if he found out that she even mentioned his name, and right now, she deserved to be punished by *Lisa,* not Griffin. *He'll never find out, so whatever.*

"I'll have to think about it then," she ended the conversation by going back into her cabin and slamming the door in Ainsling's face.

***

The next evening, a small boat arrived at *The Remnant* and two passengers were heralded on board by a big welcoming party. The Captain, Li and Mark Yancey were stunned at who Aaliyah had brought with her. Li couldn't believe it was really him- he looked so…*happy?*

Stan and Aaliyah had been lucky to make it to the ship. The car they took after leaving the yellow sports car at the station got awesome mileage. They finished the rest of their trip in six hours and made contact with *The Remnant* through the Guardian's helpers at the old church.

Stan's outfit was wrinkled and he noticed a strange smell- sweat? It had been an exciting journey, but they were ready for some rest. They unloaded their things, including the boxes Reynolds had picked up for Dr. Griffin and hurriedly stashed in the small trunk of the 'borrowed' car.

Ellen and the others lined up to greet Aaliyah and hug her or shake her hand to welcome her back. Everyone proclaimed it 'a miracle!' After Li shook Aaliyah's hand and told her how great it was that she was back, he turned to her companion and shook his hand also.

"So, you're one of us now?" He had felt Stan's bandage as he shook his hand. "How did that happen?"

"You could say I was *inspired.*" Aaliyah and he giggled. *Giggled.*

"So, how's your guitar?" He winked.

"What?" Li was confused. *My guitar?*

Wait- did Reynolds actually wink?

Seriously- this was not the same lame minion who used to follow my father around like a mindless tool...

"Well, at the time I thought I received a text from your father, telling me to deliver your guitar to a specific address. But I see the lady I gave the guitar to standing right over there, so I assume the text was really from that Guardian person."

He had pointed at Ellen and Li was amazed.

"Mission accomplished!" he yelled over to her. She gave him a thumbs-up sign. Li was staring in amazement at both of them.

Lisa walked up behind him and boldly introduced herself and welcomed Reynolds on board.

"What's in those boxes with all the warning labels on them?" She asked nosily. They all turned, looking down at the boxes together.

"I honestly don't know. But Dr. Griffin sent me to pick them up and is probably very angry I didn't return with them."

He managed to express calmness on his face despite the worry in his heart, since he'd had years of practice. Then he remembered the last time Griffin had left something dangerous in his possession, and he allowed himself to frown.

"Promise me no one will open them," he added solemnly.

"You'll never guess who else is here," Li said quietly. "Ainsling Reid- and her father!"

Reynolds was suddenly afraid.

"What?"

"Yeah, she's alive, though she is...changed."

Stan didn't comment. He knew perfectly well how changed she was. He didn't remember much of their time together after the whole cloaking incident. All he remembered was bits and pieces, visions of her and Dr. Griffin blurred together. He was now concerned he had escaped Griffin only to be caught and thrown back, like a small fish.

"She can't tell him I'm here! Li, she works for your father now!"

The Captain interrupted and assured Stan, "You are safe here, Mr. Reynolds. Ainsling is not a threat to you anymore. She is just as much of a victim as you are."

Somehow, that didn't make Stan Reynolds feel much better.

They celebrated Aaliyah's return with a small feast in a restaurant on the ship. Lisa's sister, Kayleen, had volunteered to be in charge of the food, wrangling all the Yancey girls, including Lisa, to help. Around 11 p.m., Lisa finished washing the last glass and finally sidled away from the festivities.

She was on a mission to talk to Ainsling. There were a few demeaning things she had conjured up for Ainsling to do for her. At least, for starters.

As she knocked on the door, she found it was ajar. She quietly tip-toed into the small cabin. Connor Reid was asleep on one of the beds and she heard a girl's voice coming from behind the bathroom door.

"No, nothing else, Dr. Griffin. It was another boring day. Yes, I will stay far away from him, I promise. *Wan-*"

The door flew open.

"Give me the Com," demanded Lisa, suddenly standing in front of Ainsling. When Ainsling didn't hand it to her, Lisa yanked it away and began verbally tearing into Dr. Griffin.

"Are you the mad scientist who can make people invisible? Did you also know it makes them crazy? Your guinea pig here tried to kill me and I want some retribution! You can't just let something like her loose in the world!"

"You want retribution?" he asked calmly.

"You bet I do!" she yelled back.

"Ainsling!!!"

He screeched so loudly Lisa almost dropped the Com. She held it out to Ainsling. All he said to her was,

"Grab onto that idiot...Now!"

She obeyed and held onto Lisa's elbow.

They both doubled over in pain as he activated the retribution device on his wrist. Through the air, the signal sent jolts of electricity through their bodies at a low enough intensity to let them live, but in long enough of a duration to make them *wish* they would die.

22 The Plan

There was a knock on Li's door extremely early the next morning. He reluctantly rolled out of his small bed and walked over to the door. Ellen was there. She looked as though she had come in haste. Her hair was mussed up and her eyelids appeared to be conducting a protest of their own. Li yawned first, and Ellen followed suit.

After yawning in synch, Ellen told Li the purpose of her early visit. "The Captain sent me to get you- something urgent has come up."

"Okay, let me grab a shirt." He did and then followed Ellen down the hall in a semi-conscious state.

They went into the suite without knocking, since they were expected. Occupying the room already were Aaliyah and Reynolds, Mark and Lisa, Connor and Ainsling, plus the Chief Engineer and Pastor Dave.

The group had formed an amoeba-shaped circle, filling up all the chairs, sitting on piles of books and overflowing onto the floor. Li had to force himself to look away from Ainsling. The Captain began speaking.

"There's been a message from the Guardian. I was asked to gather you all and discuss the problem together. So, here goes- a ship is coming our way. It appears we are being tracked. It has been shadowing our course for a couple hours."

A few gasps were followed by fearful silence. They waited tensely for the Captain to tell them more.

"We have a dilemma. We don't want them to catch us and risk everyone's freedom. But we can't just throw Lisa overboard or send her away in a lifeboat."

"Lisa?" asked Li, "What does this have to do with Lisa?"

All eyes turned on her.

"Well, Lisa still has a chip in her hand. It appears they are tracking it." The Captain reluctantly explained.

"Lisa! I thought you had it removed before you hurt your arm!" Ellen exclaimed. Lisa became defensive.

"Look, the Captain gave me extra time to think about it. It's not an easy choice! I never thought they would track me- I'm not important!"

"It's my fault," Ainsling said quietly. "I reported your name soon after you arrived here."

"What? That crazy Dr. Frankenstein knows my *name?*"

She shrank in fear after last night's electrical shock experience.

"So, it's been a week. Why are they acting now?" Lisa's father wondered.

Ainsling and Lisa glanced at each other. They assumed the incident last night had spurred Dr. Griffin to act. Stan had another idea.

"He must have found the car and now knows the boxes are missing."

Stan and Aaliyah exchanged knowing looks. "He is planning something bigger. The boxes I brought on board must have been part of that plan. I think he is desperate." Stan imagined Dr. Griffin's face as he discovered his supplies were missing and cringed inwardly.

"He must be very angry."

"Stan, he doesn't know where you are though! He couldn't possibly know you and the boxes are on board this ship!" Aaliyah reassured him.

She was wrong. Griffin had put two and two together and realized that Reynolds, the Guardian, Yancey, and *The Remnant* were all connected. He had sent the ship after them days ago, the night Ainsling had jogged his memory about the Guardian.

"What are we going to do, though? Can we outrun the ship?" Mark was worried, concerned about his family's safety.

"*The Remnant's* engine is satisfactory for touring, but the only way for us to outmaneuver another ship is to become a submarine. There's not a button for that in my engine room, guys! I'm not a miracle worker, you know," the Chief Engineer said sarcastically, and with a heavy Scottish accent, for some reason.

"I have an idea. We can't become a submarine, but we could *disappear*." Ainsling avoided everyone's eyes as she made her comment.

"What do you mean, Ainsling?" Ellen asked.

"I could extend my cloak to surround the ship. Then they wouldn't be able to track us," Ainsling said matter-of-factly.

"Or Lisa could take her chip out and they wouldn't have anything to track!" Li added. He looked angrily at Lisa. She bulked a little under his glare.

"Li- it's the Guardian's policy. St. Augustine inspired the premise for this rule hundreds of years ago when he wrote, '*He who created us without our help will not save us without our consent*,'" the Captain said, attempting to explain why they allowed people to choose. Free will had been as controversial then as it was now.

His words fell on deaf ears. Li remained agitated. It seemed like a foolish rule to him, despite knowing he wouldn't have liked to have been forced to join the Guardian's plan, either. This time, Lisa's freedom to choose affected all their lives!

"Ainsling, will your cloaking really make us untraceable?" Mark was doubtful.

"Dr. Griffin did tests on this kind of cloaking. As far as I could understand, the objects I extend my cloak over are just as undetectable as I am." She paused, thinking. "He *could* figure out our plan, though. This *is* his life's work in my head, you know." She tapped the side of her head. "He's not stupid."

"Will it hurt you, Ainsling?" Ellen's concern was palpable. They all turned to her in mutual concern. Connor Reid's eyes were moist. He grasped his daughter's hand.

"If it's short, like, less than two hours; I think I'll be fine," she said. Their faces showed even more concern at her uncertainty. She squeezed her father's hand.

Stan Reynolds was uncomfortable with the idea for other reasons. "Will it hurt *us?* No offence, Ainsling, but I've been cloaked by you and I had to receive electroshock therapy in order to recover from the damage it caused."

"I can control the cloak so that it affects the ship's exterior alone." She paused. "I guess I've never told you, but I'm very sorry, Mr. Reynolds. I didn't know what it would do to you then. I promise I will never harm another person like that again." He acknowledged her apology with a nod. Lisa rolled her eyes in disbelief.

Unable to hold in his frustration any longer, Li stood up.

"Or Lisa could just remove her chip!" Li repeated loudly. Lisa stood up to face him, fed up with all their blind kindness for Ainsling. *No one cared about her, just that crazy freak.*

"I don't want to take out my chip! I do not give my consent!" Lisa shot back.

They all sighed in frustration. Li rubbed his neck, leaving large red blotches peeking out from under his long, dark hair. Before he could retort again, Mark Yancey stood up.

"How could you be so selfish?" her father accused her angrily.

"Selfish?"

She laughed loosely in his face. "You should know better than anyone how to be selfish! Look, I don't *trust* this Guardian-person. I didn't ask to be brought aboard this ship and nothing has happened to change my mind about that!" She subconsciously tapped her cast.

"We can't force her. That's the rule," the Captain declared. "But we could see if there's another ship in the fleet that can meet us at the border and take her to Sector Two."

"Sector Two is more dangerous than Sector One!" Mark Yancey yelled. "We can't send her there!"

"They aren't looking for her. The trace ends at the next latitude line. What do you think, Lisa?" The Captain asked her directly and they all waited in suspense for her response.

"I'd rather go to Sector Two, where I can live my own life, than blindly trust this whacky "Guardian" because you all want me to. Like I said, I never asked to be here."

She cast a quick glance Ainsling's way.

"And I've never belonged. Take me to Sector Two," she said decisively.

Mark covered his face with his hands and felt defeated. Was this the consequence of his neglecting his family? Losing Lisa forever?

The chief engineer had been busy calculating. He shared his results with them now.

"Fortunately, the Guardian advised us to begin sailing south towards the border of Sector Two the day after Aaliyah returned. But if my calculations are correct, Ainsling, you will only have to hold the cloak over the ship for a short amount of time. The border line is forty-two nautical miles away. At twenty knots, we can be there in a little over two hours, depending on some other factors."

He went through a mental list of factors out loud. "The wind is light and coming from the North. We should be fine on fuel. I'll contact the *Blue Like Jazz* and set up a rendezvous.

They are the closest ship. They will close the distance and the time between us also, though I couldn't possibly calculate how much time that will shave off," the Chief Engineer informed them.

"Where will you need to be to do this?" the Captain asked Ainsling. She thought a minute and said, "I should go to the lowest level- in a room that's part of the hull of the ship, one that is connected to the frame. One that is reasonably quiet."

"I know just the place," the Chief Engineer replied. "I'll take you there on my way to the engine room."

"Okay, folks, let's do it! Lisa, pack lightly- you have two hours to be ready to leave. Everyone else, you are dismissed. Pastor Dave, you know what to do," he said. Dave bowed his head instantly, as if on cue. Lisa got up abruptly and left the room first.

"Ainsling, are you sure this is such a good idea?" Li was worried. His eyes had darkened and his jaw was clenched tight. She shrugged and marched past him and out the door, following the Chief Engineer's lead.

"She's risking so much," he said to the rest of the group. "I'm not sure she even cares about how it will affect her. Should we take advantage of her like this?"

He was desperate to find any excuse to drop this stupid, rotten plan.

"I'm not very happy about it, either, Li. But it's the only plan we've got. We won't leave her alone, though. Who will volunteer to go and keep her company?" the Captain queried.

The Captain watched as Connor, Li, Ellen, and Mark raised their hands immediately like school children eager to answer the teacher's question.

He smiled, the wrinkles on his forehead deepening, "Go!"

They all embarked on a mission to support Ainsling, Li leading the way.

The engine room was bustling with activity. The Chief was yelling out commands and people were running to obey. He closed his eyes for an instant and prayed for a miracle.

At the opposite end of the ship, Ainsling had made herself as comfortable as possible in the room the Chief had directed her to. She was leaning on the wall with her arms outstretched, her two hands flush against it. Li, Ellen, Mark, and Ainsling's father all paraded slowly into the room.

Ainsling was facing the wall and heard them, but didn't acknowledge their entrance. She closed her eyes and focused on her pain, on the sleeping monster inside of her. As the motley crew around her watched, her form wavered, and she vanished from their sight.

A minute later, the walls of the ship began to fade. Soon, they were as clear as glass. The room they had all gathered in with Ainsling became stealthily silent as everyone could now see into the ocean surrounding them. The gray-blue water was filled with ocean life on display. Seaweed and specks of algae were spotlighted by the brilliant rays of the morning sun into the uppermost layer of the ocean. They couldn't contain their amazement any longer.

"Hey, look- a shark!"

"A sea turtle! This is amazing! Ainsling- what a gift you have!" Ellen exclaimed.

"Wow, is this like double-sided glass? We can see out, but no one can see in?"

"It must be! That's so cool, Ainsling!"

"I'm glad you're enjoying it," a female voice announced sarcastically.

She had tried to ignore their exclamations of wonder. Their presence here was annoying and distracting. *Why had they come?*

"Quiet, everyone!" Li whispered to them. "She's got to think about bad stuff to control the cloak. You can't be acting all happy around her!"

Ellen chimed in, "Right, Li. When this is over, she's going to need us. Save your good moods for then, friends."

They all nodded in agreement and passed the time admiring the aquatic scenes showcased by Ainsling's ability in silence. Ainsling went back to work.

23 The Trigger

"Sir, we lost the signal!"

A young man in an E.C.C.O. agent's uniform looked up from his console on the bridge. The blinking dot on his screen had halted and was holding a steady red at the last known location of the chip they had been tracking. He spoke again, "We're sailing blind!"

Dr. Jay Griffin ran over to see if the pimply-faced idiot was correct. He pushed some keys and went through a few protocol checks to see if the program was malfunctioning instead of the chip. The program was functioning fine. He rubbed the back of his neck raw with frustration.

"They must have destroyed her chip!" he grumbled.

He turned to the Captain of his vessel.

"Could they have detected us at this distance?"

"No, that is unlikely. We are too far away for their limited radar capabilities. Unless they have supernatural powers, they are clueless to our presence. I'm 100% sure they never even knew we were following them."

Griffin cursed his luck. At first, he had felt hopeful. If they tracked the girl, he could recover Ainsling and eventually even Reynolds. That would lead to him reclaiming his supplies.

Now it seemed as though he would have to become invisible, too. His benefactors would not be pleased.

"Is there any way to locate them now?"

The Captain looked down at another screen. "We could take an educated guess as to their course."

"What do you mean?"

"We'll use integrated navigation theory, sir."

The doctor resigned to let the Captain take over until they located the vessel. He threatened him that if this theory that the Captain spoke of was unable to find their lost ship, there would be hell to pay.

***

The group hanging with Ainsling was sitting on the floor, whispering quietly to each other and pointing at the dark shadows in the water that had replaced the walls now. Ainsling had her back to them, though they didn't know that, since they could not see her. Their whispers wafted through the air and tickled her ears. She knew they were talking about her.

Her trigger thoughts had to be changed. Since her father was thankfully alive, now her deepest sadness came when she imagined Li doing exactly what she had told him to do- pretending she never existed.

He had been a symbol of hope for her once. She wished she could hang on to that hope. But she was not worthy of him. She would never be able to escape that fact.

This "grace" the Captain spoke of was an idealistic tease. Dr. Griffin would eventually take her away from all of them and then Li would be forced to forget her. The pain of that inevitable day strengthened the cloak, and weakened her hold on any type of hope.

Ellen stood up to stretch out her back. She hit her elbow against the wall and rolled her eyes at her own clumsiness. Yet the pain in her elbow was nothing compared to the pain in her heart.

Ainsling had been such a sweet, innocent girl when they had known each other at the hospital. This Dr. Griffin had used her to further science and his career, with no concern for the consequences. The device he had invented forced Ainsling to stay in the darkness. She had so loved the light; without it, she had lost hope.

Lisa's stubborn attitude caused her to stay in the darkness as well. They were both suffering unnecessarily. Ellen agreed with Li, Ainsling was doing this risky job out of a narcissistic need to punish herself. She also believed Lisa was spitefully running away instead of facing her problems. All of their well-intentioned advice was just empty words to her.

Words...didn't Lisa mention she had seen words written on the wall somewhere down here? Where could they be?

She wandered around the room, never venturing near the invisible wall that put the ocean world too close for comfort. She wondered if the words were on that wall. Maybe she wouldn't be able to find them, but there wasn't much else to do in the time they had to wait, so she continued to look.

In the darkest corner of the room, Ellen walked along the solid, cold wall. It was there she found the calligraphy Lisa had spoken of. The characters were not Japanese, as Lisa had guessed.

They were Chinese- a language Ellen knew well. Beautiful Chinese calligraphy filled the small wall she found. Ellen began to read it to herself.

"What are you doing?" Li said as he walked up behind Ellen. He looked at the graffiti on the wall she was studying.

"Can you read Mandarin Chinese?" she asked. He shook his head. "Not fluently. That's my father's thing. I only know a little, like numbers and stuff."

Ellen looked perplexedly at the writing.

"Oh, right, this character means 'bright'," she mused. Li shrugged his ignorance. Then he said, "My name means 'bright.'"

"No, it doesn't. 'Li' means 'strong,'" Ellen shared confidently.

"'Li' is a nickname. My real name is 'Liang,'" he told her.

She looked wistful. After a few moments in thought, she told him, "When I was a girl, I used to love the play, *The Butterfly Lovers*. It's the Chinese equivalent of *Romeo and Juliet*. Anyway, 'Liang and Zhu' were the two main characters in the story."

Li pretended to listen, but he couldn't help but be distracted by wondering how Ainsling must be suffering. He wished he could at least *see* her.

Ellen was waxing nostalgic over *The Butterfly Lovers*, unaware of Li's complete lack of interest, and continued sharing,

"Liang and Zhu couldn't be together, which destroyed Liang first, but at the end of the story, they both turn into butterflies. My grandmother used to tell me whenever you see butterflies in pairs, it was Liang and Zhu. She said- Li...are you listening?"

Li shook his head and apologized.

"It's ok, Li, I mean *Liang*. It's not important. But look at this calligraphy for a minute. Lisa told me she discovered this writing down here the day she hurt her arm.

"It's a poem written in Chinese, but it only rhymes in English. Let me translate it for you."

She read aloud, tracing the painted characters vertically with her fingers. The dark black paint was scratched and mottled.

"The days are dark, the ocean surrounds/ my fate is unseen, my fate is not ground/ For God orders all, I am just a mist/ hovering still, waiting for bliss/ the dark hides me well, my heart longs for light/ I live by this creed- it is all for the bright."

"Cool," Li said. "I guess there's a poet on board."

"Not a Chinese one. The only passengers of Chinese heritage here are you and I, Li, and I didn't write this." She looked confused.

"Well, it wasn't me! Maybe you can ask the Captain about it later. He might know of someone you don't know about."

He didn't think it was a big deal, but Ellen seemed to be seriously disturbed by it.

They wandered back to the group and sat down on the floor again. Mark Yancey's eyes had been following Li as he came back to them. He felt like this was his chance to fulfill the promise to his wife and tell Li what he knew about his mother.

He had failed his family so much. He knew Lisa's decision to go to Sector Two was partially his fault. She had always been a stubborn child, but his alcoholism must have been the final straw.

Li's childhood couldn't have been very pleasant, knowing what he knew about Jay. He noticed Li had inherited some of his mother's positive traits. *Thank God.*

"Hey, Li, can I talk to you privately?" he whispered to Li.

Li nodded and got up once again. The two walked away from the group, unwittingly towards Ainsling. Mark stopped walking and nervously asked, "How much do you remember about your mother, Li?"

"Not much. She left when I was only three years old," he said tightly. He didn't like talking about it. It still angered him to think about it.

"I knew her, you know. Your father and I worked with John at The Institute. Did he tell you?"

"John? Oh- the Captain! Yeah, he said something about seeing me as a baby, and he showed me an old picture of you all."

"Yeah, you were a cute baby. We never had any boys. My wife especially liked you, called you her little China doll. Sorry, that's probably embarrassing," he smiled in retrospect.

Li didn't comment, but looked around uncomfortably. Old people were weird sometimes.

"Anyway, John wanted me to wait to tell you this, but now that you are feeling better and we have some time, I wanted to share it with you. Actually, I *need* to tell you." Li noticed that Mr.

Yancey appeared nervous. He was sweating and kept wringing his hands together.

"Uh, okay. What is it?" Li asked nonchalantly, but was getting nervous too, as if it was contagious or something.

"Your mom didn't abandon you, Li. She had an accident." Li looked puzzled, so he continued, "She was rushed to the hospital after an exposure to ricin. It's a poisonous powder made from the castor oil plant. She recovered physically, but she lost her memory."

Li was stunned by this information. The caster... *what?*

"She lost her memory after being poisoned? Does that happen a lot?"

"No, it's not a typical side effect. It's all my own opinion, of course; but I'm pretty sure your father was behind both the ricin poisoning and the memory loss. There was never anything that obviously pointed to his guilt, but I think if you ask Mr. Reynolds, he can verify what I've always suspected." Mark grimaced at the thought of that weasel, Reynolds. He couldn't deny he felt a bit satisfied upon hearing about the effect Ainsling's cloak had had on him. He deserved a bit of suffering for his years of mindlessly serving Griffin.

"That's not all, Li. After your mother lost her short-term memory, she re-located to another city to start a new life. She even had a new name. She went by the name Elizabeth Lee. They tell patients with memory loss to start fresh with a new identity and build a new life. They help them with housing and find them a job. Your mother didn't even know she left you behind, Li."

"So- let me get this straight- she didn't leave me on purpose, she just forgot me? I don't know if that makes me feel any better, Mr. Yancey," he frowned.

"But she *did* remember! A year later, she came to our house and my wife answered the door. We were shocked to see her, but even more shocked when she told us she had regained her memory. She desperately wanted to see you- to take you with her." Li's eyes opened wide.

"We discouraged her, Li. I'm sorry. I regret it now, but, at the time, it seemed too dangerous. He tried to kill her once, Li! She must have known something she shouldn't have. If she showed up and he found out about her regaining her memory, her life and yours would have been in danger!" Mark looked pleadingly at Li.

"Please forgive me! I thought it was for the best."

"Did she just leave? She didn't even try?" he asked bitterly

"My wife took her to your house while Griffin was away so she could say goodbye to you. Mary said she cried the whole way back. It broke her heart to leave you, Li," Mark tried to say comfortingly. Li held his jaw tight, but Mark could tell he was hurt.

"I hope you can forgive me. Maybe you could have grown up with her if we hadn't discouraged her. My conscience has bothered me ever since," he said.

Li looked at him with a straight face, though his eyes were watery.

"You did the right thing. My father is a dangerous man. She was better off running from him alone. I wasn't worth the risk."

"It's hard to believe this until you have your own children, Li, but I'm telling you, even if they *want* to go away, which your mother didn't, parents are forever attached to their children." He patted Li on the shoulder and thought of Lisa.

Mark wandered back to the group, who had formed a circle on the floor in the middle of the room, leaving Li to his thoughts.

Li mumbled aloud to himself, but Ainsling had heard the whole conversation and continued to listen now. Li spoke under his breath.

"Forever attached? I wonder if that's true? Attached...like the red string... This has to stop. First my mother, and then Ainsling...My father has destroyed too many lives! I swear I will do whatever I can to get Ainsling away from him and then- I will find my mother! I can't let him hurt anyone I love ever again!"

Li's handsome, determined face was within inches of Ainsling's back. At his passionate words, her wall of anger and hopelessness came crumbling down.

The hull of the ship flickered back into view and everyone in the room gasped as they saw the ocean fading from sight, replaced with the dirty white wall of the ship once more. Li stopped in his tracks as Ainsling appeared directly in front of him. She fell to her knees and he immediately bent down to help her.

"Ainsling…are you okay?" He put his hands on her back and leaned close to her.

She breathed deeply, feeling faint. Li was there, holding her up. She could smell him. His scent was the same as before- warm, with a slight trace of sandalwood. His hands on her back were strong and comforting, clasping her securely.

How could he be so amazing? Here he was, in pain himself, yet he was still stubbornly devoted to her welfare.

"I can't do this now. I can't…" Ainsling spilled out.

Li helped her up and turned her around so she was facing him. He was shocked to see that she was smiling. To his amazement, she looked reminiscent of the Ainsling he had known a year ago- the cheerful, happy Ainsling. He reflected her bright smile with one of his own.

"You're happy?" he asked her, tilting his head. He rubbed the back of his neck, which caused her to laugh heartily.

"I've missed that laugh."

"Me, too," she responded.

They both laughed. Li hugged her. She leaned her head against his chest. When she looked up, their eyes locked.

Li gently caressed her cheek, moving over her faint freckles. They were in a world all their own. What she was feeling, here in his arms, went beyond friendship.

Ainsling realized now that it *was* love that she felt for Li. The invisible string had truly never broken, even though she had tried with all her power to cut it. Despite her hopeless state, Li had shown her what love does- always believes, constantly hopes, never leaves.

She gave Li a wholehearted kiss. A spark of electricity traveled up her spine as he returned the kiss.

Then a jolt of unyielding pain hit her. She fell out of his embrace and onto the floor.

"Ainsling!!" Li screamed. He stepped back, confused, as she writhed on the floor in agony. Then he understood. He turned to the others in the room.

"The device! My father is hurting her! They must have figured out what she was doing! Go tell the Captain that… they know!"

24 The Laughter

After running full-force all the way up the uppermost part of the ship, Mark burst onto the bridge and shouted, "Griffin knows!"

John had been bowed in prayer and was startled by the sound of Mark's scream. He looked around him, observing the frame of the huge windows had returned to view and he was no longer surrounded by what once appeared to be only blue sky, due to Ainsling's cloaking.

It had been so disconcerting, the disappearance of the walls, he had resigned himself to bow his head and pray fervently for another rescue. Now he needed to think quickly.

"How long?" he asked Mark, who was holding his side in pain from the sudden athletic effort. He spoke in bursts.

"I think it's been five minutes- but with the cloak down-"

"It'll be no time before they're on our trail again!"

Mark's lungs were on fire and he couldn't manage to breathe and talk at the same time.

"Why is the cloak down? Has something happened to Ainsling?" John asked, afraid she had exhausted herself or lost her reason again.

Mark blushed a little, his pink face blending with his red hair. "Well, apparently, she can't maintain the cloak when she is really happy."

"What's she so happy about?" the Captain prodded.

"Oh, well, let's just say it would be safe to assume Li and Ainsling are friends again. But, never mind why, what are we going to *do?*" he asked his old friend, finally able to breathe semi-normally.

"Take over for me," he commanded a member of the crew in the bridge.

He rose, reached for his cane and ambled towards the door. Mark opened it for him and they walked their way down to the room where Ainsling was. They both regretted that the elevators were all in disrepair. It was such a long walk!

They entered the room out of breath and found Ainsling whimpering in Li's arms. This time the pain from the retribution device had been the worst pain she had ever experienced. She struggled to keep herself from vomiting. Ellen tried to get her to drink some water, but she couldn't lift her head.

"Ainsling, I have to ask you some doctor type questions, try to answer as well as you can, okay?" the Captain gently explained.

She nodded.

"On a scale of 1-10, ten being the worst, how bad would you say the pain is?"

"10," she whispered. Her father was at her side, stroking her face with his scarred hand, tears dropping from his clear eyes. Her pain seemed to be felt by him in full. The Captain reverted to doctor mode. He asked the surrounding witnesses,

"How long was the initial attack?"

He needed to know if the electrical shock had done any internal damage. He sincerely hoped not, in light of their primitive medical capabilities.

Li responded, as he had been there from the start. "It was only a few seconds. She passed out after that. She woke up after Mark left, but she's still in so much pain. Can't you do anything for her?"

"It will continue to lessen. We need to keep watching her. Ellen, you're in charge of Ainsling. Li, Connor, do whatever she tells you, even if you have to go fetch something and leave her side. She'll understand," he advised.

He gave them both a compassionate look and walked to the door with Mark.

"Why don't you leave me in charge? They are all too close to her. They are too emotional." Mark looked back at the scene and sighed.

"I need you to talk to Lisa. She needs to be informed about what's happening. You need to try again at working things out with her, Mark. She's still your daughter, whether she wants to be or not," he encouraged.

Mark was afraid. He didn't have anything to say except that he was sorry and that didn't even begin to cover for his sins. No one can force someone else to forgive. It was her choice, just as leaving the chip in and going to Sector Two had been.

Reluctantly, he parted with John and went to the girls' cabin. He was welcomed in by his 15 year-old daughter, Kayleen. She greeted him happily. With a grateful heart, he remembered how his first meeting with the all his girls had lifted his spirits. Lisa appeared to be the only one unable to forgive him and start fresh.

"Is Lisa here?" he timidly asked the others. They pointed to the bathroom.

"She's back there, packing her stuff," Kayleen informed him sadly.

The idea of her going to Sector Two alone filled him with fear. Sector One was controlled by E.C.C.O., which had gradually taken away all their freedoms, but Sector Two was a political battlefield. The fighting between the two ruling parties had become outrageous and the people were so divided that it had turned into a modern twist on the Civil War.

E.C.C.O. had completely taken control of Sector One's technology, such as the Internet and all media outlets, in an attempt to circumvent the problems Sector Two experienced.

"Lisa?" he called out, "I need to speak to you. It'll just take a minute." He heard his 'father' voice come out of his mouth after months of laying in wait.

Lisa grudgingly walked out of the bathroom with a suitcase in her good hand and said in a frustrated voice, "Okay, I'll give you one minute. Go."

He wondered how Mary would handle this situation. He was never very good at confrontation. Mary had been the parent in charge most often because of all the hours he spent at his job at the Institute.

She was organized, responsible, motivational, and a skilled disciplinarian. He was goofy and fun. Mary had accused him on more than one occasion of being a kid himself. He couldn't deny he spoiled the girls. They had all the things he had never had as a child or young man growing up in tumultuous times. He regretted having pampered them now he saw how Lisa had become so incredibly selfish and ungrateful.

"Lisa, I know I keep repeating myself, but there's really nothing else I can say. I'm sorry, Lisa."

"It doesn't change anything, dad. I'm not removing my chip and I'm still leaving the ship when the time comes. You can't stop me. I can make my own decisions. I've had to take your place for the last five months. Thank you very much." Her sarcasm was grating, but he wasn't surprised at it. He decided to get to the point.

"The cloaking plan has failed. Ainsling experienced some kind of electrical shock and she can't cloak us now. They will locate us again. I thought you should know. We may not make it to Sector Two before they catch up with us. You have to prepare yourself for the possibility of our capture."

He had given her all the information. She stared at the suitcase in her hand. She was familiar with the electrical shock. Her muscles still ached from last nights' jolt.

"Is Ainsling all right?" she asked with true concern. Her revenge had been unsatisfying, to say the least, and she had begun to understand now how Ainsling was also a victim. She didn't like her, but she didn't hate her anymore.

"It seems to have been harsher than I would have expected. She passed out initially and is still in pain now, but I think she will recover soon," he said with a doctor's tone. "Li, Ellen and her father are taking care of her now."

Lisa was relieved. Ainsling's pain did not make her happy. She had once thought it would.

"Thank you for telling me what is going on. If you want to stay with us until...well, until we know more, you can. The girls are young and naïve; you might have time to earn their trust back," she said, implying she would never trust him again. Mark sighed and wondered if she would ever forgive him.

She gathered up her blanket and pillow. Then she handed them to her father.

"Take that to Ainsling first," she said, turning away from him. Carrying the bedding, he humbly left the cabin and journeyed back down towards the engine room. He ran into Stan Reynolds in the stairwell.

"Where are you going?" he asked Stan, a little haughtily. He still disliked the servile man.

"I was wondering what was going on. It appears we are *visual* again," he said flatly.

"Griffin must have figured out what we were doing. Or he just felt like hurting the girl for the fun of it. She was shocked so badly that it will be days before she is back to normal. Let me ask you something- how could you have worked for that evil man for so long? Do you have no *conscience?*" He could no longer hold in his feelings for the wretched man.

Reynolds looked ashamed.

"I did it for love," he responded simply, causing Mark to be thoroughly confused.

"Love? Are you crazy?"

"I was in love with Olivia Griffin. Of course, I never did anything about it. I have always been a coward. I know it. At first, I was willing to work for Griffin, even after I knew the truth about him, just to be near her. Then, I stayed because I thought I could protect her. After I failed to protect her and she left, I stayed because I was waiting for her to return "

His face retained a calm, straight expression during his otherwise emotion-laced confession.

Mark was speechless. This unfeeling rat had been in love with Olivia? That was even worse!

"There was Li, too. He was the only one left to remind me of her. He is more like her than he'll ever know."

"You are such a loser, Reynolds! How could you be so selfish?"

Mark stopped. The realization of how he sounded exactly like Lisa hit him in the gut. He was convicted by his own hypocrisy. They were *both* losers!

"Oh, man! What am I doing?" Mark laughed awkwardly. Reynolds looked confused.

"Seriously, I'm a pathetic alcoholic who abandoned my own children to drown my sorrows in a bottle. Who am *I* to judge *you?*"

Mark began to laugh hysterically. Reynolds assumed, due to all the stress of the day, he had lost his mind. He had some experience in that department.

"I wasn't the best friend to Olivia either. She remembered everything, you know," Mark blurted out after his laughing fit ended.

"I know that now," Stan replied. "I received a letter from her before I came on the ship." He smiled contentedly.

Reynolds' smile was still a weird sight for Mark and he struggled to keep from laughing again.

"Really? What did it say?" Mark was curious how she had lived her life. *Did she move on? Did she have a real life?*

"She told me that now was the time. I must do the right thing," he said simply.

"That's it?" Mark asked. It seemed…a bit vague. "That's all she said?"

"Yep, she wrote, 'Stanley- I have always been and will forever be your friend. Be brave- now is the time to do the right thing.'"

"She never said what the right thing was?" He was puzzled. Stanley's peace was even more puzzling. It was harder to accept than his unusual smile.

"Why aren't you disappointed? It's not like she confessed her love for you or something!"

"You don't understand. I never expected her to love me back! I'm just happy she thought of me at all! It was all I needed to hear to escape that maniac for good! Well, that and Aaliyah was a bit insistent."

This comment sent Mark over the edge and he burst out laughing again. This time, Stan joined him. They laughed together until they exhausted themselves, wiping tears from their eyes. The picture of these two grown men in hysterics was quite a comical scene.

"Look, I need to take these blankets down to Ainsling, I better-"

"I'll do it!" Stanley volunteered. He stole them out of Mark's hands before he could protest and hurried away. Mark stared after him. He felt lighter inside after this strange meeting.

***

Ainsling had rested and woke to find herself lying on a blanket on the floor of the engine room surrounded by voices. She deciphered her father's rough voice singing a song from her childhood. He could barely speak, so his efforts alone made her heart swell. She also heard Li and Ellen talking together.

There was another voice, one she didn't recognize. It was a man's voice. He appeared to be reading aloud.

"...I live by this creed- it is all for the bright!"

More discussion arose after his reading and she couldn't follow the conversation fully. Her body ached horribly, every muscle strained, as if she had just completed a 24-hour marathon.

She moaned a little as she attempted to sit up on her own. Li saw her and ran to her aid. She let him help her and leaned on him for support. Ellen and the man who had read, who she now recognized as Stan Reynolds, gathered around her, encircling her.

"How do you feel?" Ellen asked simply.

She smiled weak smile. "Tired," she answered honestly.

She squeezed her father's hand and he half smiled, his eyes lighting up. Li ran his fingers thru her hair, attempting to assemble it into some kind of style, after being flattened by the electrostatic. He was unsuccessful. This was a job better suited for Mariposa.

Ellen took her pulse and was pleased to see that it had returned to normal. Ainsling wondered how much time had passed since she let the cloak go.

"Have we been discovered?"

"No one knows yet. The Captain is on it," Ellen responded. "Let's not worry about things we can't control right now. We've been reading this random poem I found written on the wall over there. It's a worthy distraction."

"But I could try again," Ainsling said and attempted to stand up. She failed to raise herself up on her own. Her strength had disappeared.

"Stop," demanded Li, "You're done! Whatever happens, you need to rest. Let me take care of you again, like the old days. Listen to me, I'm a nurse, too!"

"Yes, sir," she saluted at him and they both smiled. Then her face turned serious.

"They must know where we are or Dr. Griffin would have shocked me again, I think."

Li frowned angrily. She was probably right. Man, he resented the fact that he was actually related to that maniac.

The Captain entered the room. Pastor Dave was with him. The group turned to them in expectation, hoping for the best, but expecting the worst.

"We are ten miles from the border. I assume we are being tracked again, but since we can't see them on our radar, they must not be that close. Ainsling, you did well. I think you bought us enough time to get away!" They all turned towards her and cheered.

"Then why do you still look so worried?" Ellen asked the Captain.

"There's a sudden storm coming at us. The sky is dark even though it's mid-morning. We're in for some rough sailing, folks." He inhaled deeply, his barrel chest expanding with air. He seemed to be bolstering himself.

Pastor Dave quoted an old hymn, "'A mighty fortress is our God- a bulwark never failing.' Let's pray our bulwarks don't fail!"

Li snickered a little. His laughter became contagious. After the strain of the last hour, they all couldn't help themselves and gave in to the moment, laughing uncontrollably.

"*Bulwark!* That's the funniest word I've ever heard!" someone shouted.

"Hey guys, this is serious!" Dave attempted to calm them, but failed miserably, as he also began to giggle like a little girl, and set them all off in another round of stress-relieving hysterics.

25 The Letters

"There's a sudden storm approaching from the west! It looks bad," yelled the pubescent-looking E.C.C.O. agent.

Jay Griffin peered over his shoulder at the weather satellite image and saw the storm that had suddenly appeared over the ocean on the screen.

He had been inwardly celebrating the return of the signal from Lisa's chip after his experimental shocking of Ainsling. Apparently, she had been cloaking her, as he had begun to suspect.

He wavered between pride in his invention and annoyance that it had been used against him. She had almost fooled him. He didn't think she had it in her, but he figured it couldn't hurt to check, at least, it wouldn't hurt *him*. The second after pushing the buttons simultaneously on his wristband, the signal returned.

They had been slowly overtaking the ship and now they had to overcome a new obstacle- an obstacle he had no control over- the weather. He gritted his teeth and left the bridge to search the skies for the approaching storm. One of the crew followed him as he walked at a brisk pace, headed for the outer deck.

"Sir, you should remain in the enclosed area during a storm like this!"

"Don't tell me where I can and can't go. I can go wherever I want to, you idiot!" He was so sick of having to rely on this inept crew.

He burst through a door leading outside. The robin egg blue sky was perfectly clear. In the distance, he heard a slight rumble. He sighed impatiently. *Imbeciles!* That storm was far away! It couldn't stop them from overtaking *The Remnant*!

***

The Captain and Ellen were sitting in the bridge, overlooking the sea before them. Ellen was deep in thought. John leaned over and waved his hand in front of her face. She blinked quickly and shook her head, laughing a little.

"Sorry, I was thinking," she explained.

"I could see that. What's got your mind working overtime?"

"I found something interesting down in the engine room today, John."

It was unusual for her to call him by his first name. He noticed it and looked at her quizzically. She was grasping a white piece of paper tightly in one hand.

"Is that it?" he pointed at the mysterious piece of paper. She handed it to him and he began to read it.

"It was initially written in Chinese calligraphy, John." As he continued reading it, tears welled up in his light gray eyes. He gently laid it down on his lap and looked longingly out the big window, as if he could see more than churning clouds in the sky above.

"Was Liang's mother ever a passenger on *The Remnant*?"

John turned to look her in the eyes and told her the truth.

"Not a passenger, a guest."

"What? I don't understand. Why haven't you told him?" she asked, confused. "He might want to know whatever you can tell him about her."

"It's not my call, Ellen. Look, I can't talk to you about it right now. Please don't ask me any more questions."

His response left her with no choice but to be silent. She accepted he must have his reasons and she trusted him.

The storm had found them. They saw the dark waves beginning to rise higher and higher, the white froth was evidence of the violence of their motions. The wind whipped around the ship and made ghoulish screams that were heard through the thick windows. Ellen caught herself clutching the sides of her chair until her knuckles had turned white. John hold tightly onto his cane and they sat together in silence as they watched the turbulent storm.

***

Stanley Reynolds admired Li as he took care of Ainsling. He had propped her head up with a pillow and guarded her like a stone wall as she slept.

Olivia would be so proud of him, he thought. Despite having a lonely childhood, and a father who treated him like a commodity, he had somehow learned how to love. It was amazing how it had changed him.

Li was cognizant of Reynolds' eyes watching him. He began to feel uncomfortable and attempted to make small talk in the hope he would stop staring.

"How's your cabin, Reynolds?"

"Oh, it's comfortable, thank you, sir." Li felt more uncomfortable after being called 'sir' and said, "Just call me Li, Reynolds."

"Then call me Stan. Aaliyah says 'Stanley' sounds like a 'grandpa-name,' so just call me Stan."

Li laughed because he could totally imagine Aaliyah saying that. As he looked down at Ainsling once more, Li remembered Mark had mentioned he should ask Stan about his father's involvement in his mother's accident. He needed to know for sure. This seemed to be as good a time as any.

"Mark told me what he believes about what happened to my mother, Stan. Do you know- Well, what I mean to say is…did my father hurt her?"

Li's face looked so young to Stan. He was still a kid. A kid who had been alone and lived without a real parent for too long. He knew he deserved to know the truth.

"Yes. I was there. If I hadn't been so naïve, it never would have happened. She told me she was planning to leave your father and she needed something, well, to hold against him, or else he would destroy her, and you, too. It sounds like she was a terrible person, but she was right. Your father would never have let her leave him without a fight. She wanted to protect you." Stan had never spoken so openly like this to Li.

"I gave her an envelope that held a file which would implicate your father in a crime. I didn't know he had contaminated it with poison! It's all my fault. It should have been me! She could have died, all because of my stupidity!" Li could feel his regret and saw it clearly in his formerly vacant looking eyes.

"It's my father's fault, not yours, Stan. Did he have something to do with her amnesia?" he asked, hoping to help Stan to move past depreciating himself.

"He confessed to me before I left that he used his own special version of electroconvulsive therapy on her that caused her memory loss, but I had always suspected him of tampering with her brain. It was hard to watch her leave, but without the memory of what happened, she was safe. You were safe." He sighed.

To Li's amusement, Stan's stoic face suddenly lit up like a light bulb.

"Li, I have good news, though! Your mother…she is still alive! Look, here is a letter I just received from her!"

He handed the precious correspondence to him. Li held it as if it was made of glass. He gradually found the nerve to open it gently and read it. It was succinct and inspiring. He read through it again.

"She sounds nice," he said with emotion.

Stan responded tenderly, "She was the nicest person I ever met."

"How did you get this letter? Through the mail? Was there a return address?"

The note appeared to have been folded and re-folded in various different ways. The colorful paper was marred by the fuzzy lines crisscrossing it. Li wondered about the possibility of locating her.

"No, Aaliyah told me the Guardian sent someone personally to deliver this message in a sealed envelope. It was someone at the sanctuary church. I am grateful she even thought of me after all these years. I owe her so much!"

He smiled like a child with a new toy. Li understood completely. It was an answer to prayer.

As if responding to the mention of her name, Aaliyah walked over to join them. She gave Stan a lop-sided grin.

"Are you talking about me, Mr. Suit?" she joked.

"Maybe," he joked back, with a hint of flirtation.

So weird! Li thought to himself. He was amazed at the difference in him. *I guess we've all changed.* But Stan's change was the most obvious. He would have once compared him to a statue, but now, he was alive. Like Pinnochio after the Blue Fairy granted his wish, he was a real boy.

"Aaliyah, do you remember who gave you the letters from the Guardian?" Stan asked.

"She was a thin, Asian woman with long black hair at the church. She told me her name was 'Elizabeth,' but she could have made it up."

"An Asian woman?" Stan looked thoughtful.

"Wait- did you say 'Elizabeth'?" Li interjected. *Didn't Mark tell him earlier that his mother had changed her name to 'Elizabeth Lee?'*

"Aaliyah, Stan- I think that was my mother!"

"Your *mother?* Wow, that seems unlikely, Li. Hey, is that the letter from your envelope, Stan?"

She was pointing at the origami paper with the handwritten note scribbled on it that Li was now holding.

"Can I look at it?" She deferred to Stan. He nodded his approval and slowly held out the precious correspondence.

She gingerly examined the colorful square of paper flipping it over and over. She appeared intrigued by the hand-penned writing.

"Guys, this is weird. *My* message was from the Guardian and *yours* was from Olivia, right?"

Stan nodded again.

"This paper is so similar...how many people do you know write letters on origami paper? And, I'm no expert, boys, but I think this is the same handwriting."

They all were stunned.

"Does this mean that...my mother...?"

Li paused. Stan finished for him.

"Your mother, Olivia...is the Guardian."

26 The Question

"The other ship is showing up on the navigational radar, Captain. It's close now," the Chief Engineer informed him. "But this storm is getting worse. We can't navigate through it. We'll have to wait it out!"

The Captain understood. He let the engineer get back to his duties. He had come in person to tell him this bleak news.

The bridge became unsafe for Ellen and him to remain in, so they rose to leave. Before vacating the room, Ellen scanned the ocean and spotted a white speck in the distance through the darkness of the storm.

"Is that the ship that's following us?" she asked the Captain. He squinted his eyes in the direction she was pointing. It had to be the one.

They watched it a few minutes more. It started as a speck, but soon became larger. They could almost make out its shape. Ellen's heartbeat pounded in her ears as her fear increased. She wondered what would happen to all of them if E.C.C.O. caught them. Would they be tortured? Imprisoned? Would she ever see her friends- her *family*- again?

All of a sudden a bright light lit up the sky and was accompanied simultaneously by a tremendous clap. They watched as a stream of light extended from the sky in a crooked line and connected with the ship in the distance. Ellen gasped. The Captain watched as smoke rose from the boat. The cloud of smoke was accented by red light, which he assumed was fire.

"We need to leave the bridge-now!" the Captain shouted to Ellen.

"Chief, get us away from this storm!" Without hesitation, the Chief replied, "Aye, Captain!"

He pushed a button that sounded a warning alarm throughout the ship, and then left as quickly as possible. The Captain took long strides with his cane.

He and Ellen headed below the main deck to his quarters and were stopped by a huge group of people desperate to know why the alarm was going off. They were beginning to panic.

"What was that noise?" asked one.

"How bad is the storm?" said another.

"Do we have enough lifejackets?" worried one more.

The questions grew more and more frantic, as the passengers were overtaken by fear. The Captain raised his cane up in the air and waited for them to calm down.

"The noise you heard was thunder. The ship that was following us has been struck by lightning. It is on fire. We are helpless to assist them in this tumultuous weather."

"Assist them? Are you crazy?" a man shouted.

"Right now, they are just as in need of a rescue as you all once were! Now, please, go to your cabins, put on the lifejackets you will find in the emergency kits in your closets and pray we don't meet the same fate! Storms at sea are unpredictable. The Chief is doing his best, but I can't promise anything. I'm not going to lie to you. Anything is possible."

Being a stern leader when necessary, he had said what they needed to hear. The passengers of *The Remnant* left to follow the Captain's instructions, appropriately respectful of both the Captain and the storm.

"Captain, I really need to speak with you." Li's voice from behind him.

He turned and saw him standing there with a weak Ainsling, who was being pushed in a wheelchair by Stan Reynolds. Aaliyah had also accompanied them.

"It's a bad time, Li."

"Really? I hadn't noticed!"

The Captain was puzzled by Li's angry face. He was fuming.

"Come on in," he replied, opening the door for them all. Ellen didn't know if she should stay, but awkwardly followed the small group into the suite. She absconded to the kitchenette area and assumed the responsibility of making tea for everyone. The others sat on the chairs and couch as they had earlier that morning.

"What's on your mind, Li?"

Stanley and Aaliyah set two pieces of colorful square paper on the coffee table. He picked them up and examined them. He soon realized why they were here.

"So you know now?" he resigned.

"That my mother is the Guardian?" Li stood up, rubbing the back of his neck vehemently. His face was twisted with hurt.

"How could you not tell me? You must have known this whole time! It's been over a year, man!"

"It was not *my* choice," he said plainly. He bowed his head in shame.

"Your mother made me promise to keep her identity a secret until the right time came. I couldn't tell anyone! It has torn me up inside, Li, watching you suffer and grow up without knowing her- without knowing that she has been watching over you all your life."

"Why does she want to keep it a secret? Wait- 'watching over me? How?"

Anger and disappointment mixed on his face, which was reminiscent of the first time Ainsling saw him that day at the Clinic when she had referred to him as 'the angry boy.' Ainsling reached out and gently placed her hand on his arm. His skin was hot.

Ellen overheard everything and couldn't help but interject, "It makes sense now! The poem, Li- 'It is all for the bright…' The bright- meaning you, *'Liang'!*"

She looked compassionately at his hurt face, hoping this realization would comfort him somehow.

"Li, she's kept her reasons to herself. She may tell you why someday, but I certainly have no right to know," the Captain said. Stan hung his head down and covered his eyes with his hands.

"Something happened to her, though, Li. Something big. Why else would she find people with broken hearts and lives and bring us all together for one purpose- rescue.

"Your mother and I barely knew each other when I worked at The Institute with your father. I heard the rumors about her accident. After I had to fire him, of course, I was very suspicious about what had happened to her."

"Years later, I received a call from someone who was interested in buying my old boat. I didn't realize it was her for some time. She had a new name, Elizabeth Lee. She was a wealthy investor and recruited me to be a Captain for her fleet of tour boats. A year later, she informed the whole fleet's employees about her real ambition. That's when we joined her in the rescue business."

John took a deep breath. This was *his* story. He didn't consider it a betrayal of his promise to share it with them now that they had discovered who she really was. He believed Olivia would approve. Wasn't it possible that she had deliberately put these pieces of the puzzle in place in the hope they would put them together and discover her identity on their own?

"We all believed in her because she had believed in us. So, we removed our chips- and that was how *I* was rescued, Li. Helping others on *The Remnant* kept me from living in despair. Before she found me, I was a wreck. When she thought the time was right, she sent the order for us to rescue you."

"You said I was being rescued from 'The Devil'- my father," Li remembered.

John dared to reveal more information. Elizabeth/Olivia had once answered his own questions on the matter. He felt Li should know. Olivia might be upset with him, but he was willing to face the consequences. She was a forgiving person.

"You were. Did you know your mother was a veterinarian, Li?"

"Yeah. So what?" he retorted.

"So, the chips E.C.C.O. forced on everyone are based off the design of the chips once used solely for pets. Olivia never trusted your father. She didn't tell me how she managed to do it, just that she implanted one of those old pet chips into each of you. I believe she said it was in your neck."

Li lightly touched the back of his neck.

"She always knew where you were and was watching over you, in the only way she could, through the years. I wish she had told me why she waited so long to rescue you, but she didn't."

"Can I talk to her? Can I see her?"

The Captain looked at Li with sympathy. He thought of Li as the son he never had. All the good deeds he had tried to do over the years hadn't assuaged his guilt. Only his faith in a forgiving God had done that. Olivia had given him a purpose and the time to discover that truth. He wondered if Li would continue to seek God after he answered his question.

"I'm sorry, Li, she hasn't been on this ship for a very long time. I honestly don't know where she is. I don't think she can risk the exposure." Li's face fell upon hearing this.

"Though there are a lot of things she doesn't explain to me, I respect your mom too much to doubt her now, Li. Try to understand- she wants the best for you. She still loves you very much."

Stan had tears streaming down his face and Li looked shell-shocked. Ellen was quietly weeping and Aaliyah hung her head sadly.

Ainsling was the only one who had maintained her composure. She leaned her head on Li's arm as he stood beside her wheelchair.

"She must miss you an awful lot, Li." Ainsling grasped his hand and looked at him sympathetically.

"Maybe. I just want to hear her voice, but she's hiding from me! What do I do now?"

His eyes met the Captain's and they both knew what the other was thinking. The Captain bowed his head first, followed by Li, at first reluctant, then resigned.

They prayed aloud for Li, for the future and for the present danger. Ainsling wondered what this was all about. Why did it bring a noticeable peace to everyone to do this?

Li concluded with a faint, "Amen."

He looked down at Ainsling's face.

Her radiant smile had finally returned and here she was, by his side again. Despite his disappointment in his mother's elusiveness, he couldn't deny he was surrounded by a lot of wonderful people.

There was the Captain- who had been not only his friend, but his mentor, perhaps a father as well.

Still as understanding and compassionate as the day he met her on the Metro covered in a patchwork knitted scarf, Ellen had treated him as her own son and made him feel cared for. He suspected she had a hole in her heart after losing her baby and he was honored to be a temporary fill.

Stan had left his cowardly self behind. He was visibly transformed. Aaliyah was constant and steadfast- a rock of strength. She was a survivor, an inspiration.

"It's gonna be all right," he declared and smiled confidently, "Maybe it won't be easy, but I am thankful to be here with all of you."

Ainsling had somehow known this was what Li had been meant to be from the beginning- not angry, but good. She felt a connection with his mother at that moment. His mother, the Guardian, after all, had given him his name.

Liang- bright, good.

27 The Guardian

Ellen was now alone in the Captain's quarters. The storm left as quickly as it came. The ship that had been following them had completely caught fire. While they had been talking in the Captain's quarters, the ship had sunk into the deep ocean.

After the difficult conversation about Li's mother, or the Guardian, they had been informed by the Chief about the sunken ship.

On the same day Li had found out the truth about his mother, his father had died. Ellen wondered how he was taking the news. Was there a part of him that would be sad about the loss? She had no idea what it must feel like to have a father like that.

The Captain had gone to talk with Lisa. Since they were no longer being tracked, they needed to decide what to do next. She could decide to stay or continue to run to Sector Two. Ellen hoped she would stay. She had seen so much change in people after their rescue; she wanted Lisa to allow herself to be changed and experience the joy she felt.

She collected the tea things and was wiping off the coffee table when she noticed the letters were still there. She picked them up to put them somewhere safer, and saw the paper had many folds, though the creases had been flattened out.

As a little girl, her grandfather had taught her the art of origami. She picked up the paper and recognized the mountain and valley folds. Stan's letter was written on a one-sided blue checked paper. In Chinese tradition, the color blue represents honor and faith. It can also represent a bond of the spirit. Aaliyah's letter was green, which is the traditional color of healing, representing growth and strength.

She sat down with the blue paper and began to recreate the folds. After a few minutes, Stan's letter became a fish, traditionally a symbol of happiness and freedom. She smiled at the message within the paper the Guardian had given Stan - a faithful bond of the spirit of freedom.

Aaliyah's letter had once been folded into the form of a cat, the symbol of independence and of a strong protector. She smiled as she thought of how well this suited Aaliyah.

Ellen bowed her head in honor of the Guardian. She was so grateful for her own rescue, and tears filled her brown eyes as she thought about how many other lives had been given a second chance because of her efforts. She had sacrificed much, including a life with her only son, but she had succeeded in making a difference.

Ellen vowed she would continue to be like a mother to Li so he would feel Olivia's watchful care for him through her. Li's mother would someday return to him, she was certain.

How had her life led her to this place? It was not of her own doing. This God the Captain loved to talk about- was that the answer? If so, what would God do next for her and the passengers of *The Remnant*?

***

Stan and Aaliyah strolled along the upper deck. The air after the storm was crisp, as if it had been wrung out and dried. The stars above the deep inky sea shined bright enough to cast dotty reflections on the surface of the water. It was as if either the sky or the ocean had doubled and encapsulated them.

Stan hadn't said much since the meeting at the Captain's quarters, not that he was particularly loquacious, but Aaliyah sensed he was preoccupied. Aaliyah was still trying to comprehend it all herself. Finally, she was the first to break the silence.

"Olivia...has a nice smile," she said, remembering the slender, simple woman from the church basement. She leaned on the railing.

To her surprise, Stan came alongside her, placed his hand over hers and replied, "So do you."

***

Connor Reid held his daughter's hand as Li pushed her wheelchair back to his cabin. He was so glad she was no longer in danger from that terrible man, Dr. Griffin. His ship had burned and then sunk into the vast ocean.

The scars that covered his face, throat, and parts of the right side of his body seemed to throb again as he imagined it. Fire is not discriminating, he had learned.

Connor wished his throat had not been injured by his own experience with fire so he could speak words of comfort to the boy.

He liked him. Once he thought his daughter would never have hope again- would never be the happy, optimistic teenager she had been before the covert surgery. But Li had touched her heart and pulled her back. It was as if they were connected somehow.

He wanted to tell Ainsling he had felt that same way about her mother. He turned his wedding band around on his finger and his enduring love for her give him strength even now.

This was the reason he had never given up hope, even in the darkest of times. He had known true love. It outshone the sadness of his life that began when he lost her in that unexpected accident all those years ago, when Ainsling was just a baby, and his wife merely a humble nanny.

He strode quietly alongside Ainsling's wheelchair and followed Li towards their cabin. Once they arrived, he shooed them both off, excused himself, and closed the door. They needed time to talk alone.

Once the door had closed, Ainsling giggled. Li couldn't express how much he loved that sound. She was still pale, but he noticed she had gained some coloring in her cheeks in the short time since her painful ordeal that morning.

The news about his mother had been frustrating, and yet, he felt more hope than he had ever felt before. He didn't know how he was going to wait for his mother. It seemed he was always waiting.

But the fact his father couldn't hurt Ainsling anymore gave him some relief. And Ainsling needed him again. He had a promise to fulfill.

They made their way to Li's cabin and he escorted her inside. Once there, Li began searching the room for something. Ainsling's eyes watched him pilfer through drawers and bags. Finally, he pulled out what he had been hunting so desperately for- a red ball of yarn.

He unwrapped a length of it and cut it. Reaching down, he wrapped it around her ankle and knotted it firmly. He looked up at her from the floor. She smiled brightly down at him. She put her hand on his head and ran her thin fingers through his thick, dark hair.

"Good boy," she recited. He stood up in front of her and chided teasingly, wagging his finger at her,

"Don't ever try to cut me out of your life again! Now you know it'll never work, right?"

Ainsling nodded, laughing her old laugh, which made Li happier than anything else in the world, and then turned serious as she looked up from her wheelchair into his warm, brown eyes.

"Your mother is the Guardian," she stated simply. He took a deep breath and let it out slowly.

"Crazy, huh?"

Ainsling could tell he was at peace though. She took his hands in hers and squeezed them. He squeezed back, then leaned over and kissed her.

This kiss was pure and untainted by tragic circumstance, pain, or guilt.

It was simply love.

Epilogue

The square room was dark with shadows and the sunlight was fighting to sneak in past the blinds. A bland, antiseptic smell permeated the air. The rhythmic beeping from a machine was in sync with the green line of peaks and valleys created on the machine's display.

"How is he?" a gruff voice asked mechanically.

"Nothing has changed. You should be glad he's not a vegetable."

The doctor didn't answer.

The cantankerous nurse continued, "He doesn't even know his own name. Maybe after some serious therapy, we can recover some of his memory."

The short man in light blue scrubs continued to nurse the patient and checked his I.V. drip. Amazingly, there were no outward physical signs of damage on the middle-aged man sleeping on the bed.

As soon as the doctor had been alerted to his recovery, he traveled as quickly as possible to retrieve him first. After spending three days in a life raft floating in the open sea, the man suffered from neurocognitive deficits and dehydration. They were lucky he had even survived.

"Hey- what's this thing on his wrist? It's completely charred, yet his skin isn't burnt. Why didn't they remove it earlier?"

The older man inspected it. He couldn't find a clasp, or any way to remove it.

"Must be a watch or a bracelet. I wonder if he can tell us anything about it, or if he will ever remember. I need *something* to investigate. We don't even know where his lab is!"

The gruff man's jaw was firm as he gritted his teeth in frustration. He stared at the bracelet intensely.

"If we could locate his lab and open his files, we could reproduce the device and the serum ourselves."

They both frowned at the immobile, seemingly innocuous form sleeping on the hospital bed. They left the tiny room and walked down the dimly lit hallway. The stern man slowed to a stop.

His companion, the short nurse, guessed where his thoughts lay. "Any news on the girl?"

"The cruise ship they were tracking is long gone by now. Don't worry, we are developing another plan."

The man evenly stroked his white beard, and declared,

"She's the key to everything- we must find the girl."

About The Author

Diane Marie Prokop was born in Pennsylvania. She is a singer-songwriter and avid knitter. Diane and her family now reside in Houston, Texas along with four cats and much yarn. The Red String is her first novel.

Connect online:
https://www.facebook.com/daysoftheguardian
https://daysoftheguardian.wordpress.com

Made in the USA
Columbia, SC
20 January 2018